I have two boyfriends . . . both good-looking with great personalities. How can I make up my mind which one to keep and which one to drop?

In her new role as teen guru for the local news-paper, Hatty is up against some pretty tough questions – acne, over-protective parents, a troublesome love-life. No question is too curly for the *Hotline*.

But who does Hatty turn to in moments of crisis? Just how does *she* deal with a mountain of mail, a step-grandmother who's obsessed with garden gnomes, and a boyfriend who's fed up to the back teeth?

Find out in the hilarious sequel to *Sit Down, Mum, There's Something I've Got To Tell You* – another misadventure with the (in)famous Hatty Duncan.

Hatty's Hotline

MOYA SIMONS

Puffin Books

Puffin Books
Penguin Books Australia Ltd
487 Maroondah Highway, PO Box 257
Ringwood, Victoria 3134, Australia
Penguin Books Ltd
Harmondsworth, Middlesex, England
Viking Penguin, A Division of Penguin Books USA Inc.
375 Hudson Street, New York, New York 10014, USA
Penguin Books Canada Limited
10 Alcorn Avenue, Toronto, Ontario, Canada M4V 3B2
Penguin Books (N.Z.) Ltd
Cnr Rosedale and Airborne Roads, Albany, Auckland, New Zealand

First published by Penguin Books, 1997
This edition first published, 1997
3 5 7 9 10 8 6 4 2

Typeset in 11/14pt Bookman by Midland Typesetters
Made and printed in Australia by Australian Print Group

National Library of Australia
Cataloguing-in-Publication data:
Simons, Moya, 1942– .
Hatty's hotline
ISBN 0 14 038472 3.
I. Title
A823.3

For Mum – 'the best is yet to be'

Chapter One

Joe Litta's my stepdad, though I'm still getting used to it, because he only married Mum six weeks ago.

They tied the knot in our back garden. A celebrant, who was allergic to our wattle tree, stood in front of Mum and Joe and, in between sneezes, married them (to each other, that is). Joe had his straight brown hair neatly combed and wore a tuxedo with a red carnation in his lapel. Mum wore a cream-coloured dress and a hat with a tiny veil.

I was the bridesmaid. I stood behind them wearing a yellow silk dress and holding a small bouquet of white roses.

'You look like a lemon meringue pie, Fatty Hatty,' said Weasel. He's Suzy's painful little brother. In a moment of misplaced kindness, Mum invited him to the wedding along with Suzy, my best friend, and Giles, her boyfriend. Raymond, my true love, a tall, lean guy with sensitive eyes and a sensitive soul, came too.

I don't think I'd have coped otherwise. What with Mum and Joe so thrilled they were crying, and Joe's mum and relatives blowing their noses, bawling in each other's arms, saying how it was just the happiest of happy days.

My dad lives in New Zealand, so I only get to see him from time to time. That makes Joe a stand-in for the real thing. Nobody told me that getting a stepfather would be such an adjustment. It was one thing for Joe to have dated Mum all those months. He went home after the dates. Now, when he's not working at his office, he's around the house annoying me.

He cracks his knuckles. I don't remember him doing *that* when he dated Mum. And he uses a toothpick after each meal. That's a habit he acquired after he married Mum, too. Mum and I have healthy gaps between our teeth, so what would we know about toothpicks? Joe delicately picks the food out of his teeth and then arranges the scraps on his empty plate. Then he peers in amazement at the tiny mounds of neatly stacked meat and potato. What can be going on in his mind?

And he spends ages in the bathroom. And he has this awful habit of not putting the lid down on the toilet seat. Then there's the way his lower jaw twitches when he's feeling emotional. It quivers like a bowl of nervous jelly.

It's not that I don't like Joe. Despite his obnoxious habits he's quite good-natured and friendly, and an excellent cook. He's kind too, and once liberated a cockroach. He flushed it down the toilet three times, and when it re-emerged after each flush, groggy but alive, he decided to return it to the wild. He scooped it up and released it in a moving ceremony at the end of the garden.

Joe's kind of grown on me, a bit like a friendly fungus. And he genuinely likes me, despite the way I growl at him. But, hey, I'm almost fourteen and three-quarters. It's a difficult age. And Joe's forty-six and three-quarters and he's never had kids. What does he know about sensitive teenagers?

Then there's his mum, Kathryn. She's a tiny person with wispy grey hair twisted into a bun, skinny cheeks and a big mouth. She's very happy that Joe finally married. So she moved from the retirement village where she lived, to a little flat just a sneeze down the road from us.

Mum and I used to have the house all to ourselves. Now suddenly there's Joe, who's everywhere at all times, and Kathryn. She visits all the time, and does irritating things like re-arranging the cushions Mum and I have casually scattered on the sofa.

'I think yellow cushions always reflect more sunlight when placed in the centre of the sofa,' she says.

'Oh, yeah?'

'Your beef stew is delicious, Margaret, but if you'd add just a touch of pepper I do think it would enhance the flavours, dear.'

'Oh, yeah?'

'Let me arrange the linen cupboard for you, Margaret,' she tells Mum, then, before Mum has time to blink, she's attacking it, colour co-ordinating all the towels and sheets in neat piles facing due north.

'Mum's swell, isn't she?' beams Joe, after his mother cheerfully waves us all goodbye. 'Isn't it wonderful the way she comes to visit all the time?'

Mum smiles and says, 'She's lovely, Joe. And yes, it's wonderful the way she comes to visit all the time.'

Generally speaking, Mum's a very honest person. She won't even let me eat half a Mars bar while we're queuing at the supermarket checkout, saying, 'It's not ours, Hatty, until we've paid for it.'

So, it's interesting to see her now, fumbling with her fingers, and to watch her nostrils flaring – a dead giveaway on those rare occasions when she tells a whopper.

I decide to go over to Raymond's house. It's Saturday afternoon. That means his dad's band will be practising. They've got a gig this Sunday at Watsons Bay in the garden of the hotel there. They're playing under a big blue awning, while families sit at tables in the hot sun and stuff themselves with fish and chips.

I leave the house, cut through the park, and arrive at Raymond's house. I push open the creaking gate attached to the white picket fence and stroll along the path to the front door. The garden is filled with lots of rainbow-coloured petunias.

Mrs Dobie, Raymond's mum, opens the door. Today she's wearing jeans, but some-times she wears a sari. She's from India and has a red painted dot in the middle of her fore-head. While my skin freckles in the sun, hers remains beautifully coffee-coloured.

Mrs Dobie's fun but a bit absent-minded. Once, she was frying onions when the phone rang. She carried on talking and it was only when the house became foggy with smoke that she realised the kitchen was on fire.

Raymond's dad is from Scotland. He says he's descended from a long line of Scottish kings, through an ancient lady-in-waiting who was keen on a Scottish king. He says that one day he'll lead his own army into Scotland and reclaim his crown. He also thinks I'm terrific because I'm so keen on jazz.

'Come in, Hatty.' Mrs Dobie smiles at me. I follow her into the sunroom at the back of the house. The drummer is just setting up his drums and Mr Dobie is playing a few scales on his clarinet. The guitarist is plucking the strings of his guitar. Raymond is bent over the piano, his dark wavy hair falling in an exceptionally cute way over one side of his face. His eyes are like two lumps of coal as they bore into the piano keys, while his long fingers stroke the keys lovingly.

'Let's try "Sweet Georgia Brown",' he calls out to his dad. My very favourite. Okay, it may not be considered cool for Raymond and I to like old songs, but we're crazy about jazz and this is our song.

Raymond sees me, jumps up from his piano stool and quickly walks over to me, giving me a casual kiss on the cheek. Mrs Dobie shakes her head and says, 'You two'.

If she thinks that peck is something, she should see us in action. Raymond is a very meaningful person and his kisses really are intensely passionate and sensitive. I should know.

I plonk myself on a beanbag. Mrs Dobie, who makes the most eye-watering curry this side of India, has baked Anzac biscuits. She puts a large plate of them on the floor next to me and, being greedy, I take two.

'I accidentally put curry powder in the mixture,' says Mrs Dobie. 'But don't worry. I put in a lot of golden syrup to make up for it.'

Immediately, I put one biscuit back, and nervously bite into the other, while Mrs Dobie smiles encouragingly at me. The biscuit tastes like curried sugar. I don't think my taste buds will ever be the same again. While I run to the kitchen to get a glass of water to put out the syrupy flames, the band starts up and begins to swing.

I go back to the sunroom and sit next to Mrs Dobie. She offers me another Anzac, but I politely tell her that too much golden syrup brings me out in hives.

I watch Raymond. His hands, hovering like nervous bungee jumpers, spring onto the keyboard. His dad's fingers crawl around the clarinet playing clear, beautiful music. The guitarist's eyes glaze over as he strums. The drummer drums. The beat makes me click my fingers and tap my feet.

Later, Raymond walks me home and we cut through the park. A few weeks ago I asked Raymond if he'd make a point of kissing me beside every tree in the park. Naturally, he said yes. I mean, who wouldn't? I'm a very good, meaningful kisser. There are twenty-seven trees in the park but I read in the local paper that there's going to be a big tree planting program there. In a short time there'll be over a hundred trees. Imagine. We could set some kind of record.

Raymond says to me, 'You know, Hatty, I really want to make it big on the jazz scene. Maybe when I've finished school I could go overseas. Dad's got connections in Scotland and maybe I could find work with a band.'

Raymond's dark eyes gleam like two shiny prunes as he daydreams. I wave my hand in front of his eyes.

'Hey, remember me?'

He puts an arm around me. 'Look, Hatty, I don't know exactly when I'll be able to go. But I want to go sooner or later. I want to see the world. You could come. We could go together. Visit England and Scotland and the States and Europe . . .'

'And even sail down the Nile to the Valley of the Kings,' I finish. Then I start to think. 'I guess I'll have to start saving – but how? You earn money from your gigs with the band, but I've just got my pocket money. I'll have to find a job.'

'You're smart, Hatty. There are so many things you can do. You'll come up with something. And then one day, we'll go. Maybe, anyway.'

That's Raymond. He's deep and complicated

and wants to be a great jazz pianist, but he needs me to give him some support and encouragement because he doesn't realise how terrific he is.

'No maybes, Raymond,' I say. 'We'll do it. It's no good having a dream if you can't make it come true.'

Raymond leaves me at the front gate. I go inside the house. I can hear the whirr of the blades as Joe cuts the grass outside. I walk along the hall to the kitchen and wave to Aunt Harriet and her boyfriend Thomas hanging on the wall. Their picture, that is. I'm named after Aunt Harriet.

She was in love with Thomas but he had this fling with a floozy and it put a big dent in his romance with Aunt Harriet. She became a nurse with the Red Cross but unfortunately got flattened by a tank after a post-war party, at the end of World War II. I like to talk to Aunt Harriet from time to time, though I'm a bit embarrassed to do it when Joe's around.

Hey, if I get to go to Normandy in France I'll be able to see the spot where Aunt Harriet got flattened. I can say nice words about her right where it happened.

I sniff the air. That good smell is Joe's satay chicken. He's a very good cook, our Joe. Now, if I can just get him to stop cracking his knuckles and studying his toothpickings.

I open the back door and look at the scene in the garden. Joe's pushing the lawn-mower and is wearing a pair of shorts and a t-shirt. He has very skinny legs and bumpy, bony kneecaps. There are big sweat patterns on the t-shirt. Mum has a floppy sun-hat on and she's putting fertiliser around the flower beds. Her cheeks are bright red and her light brown hair falls softly around her face.

It all looks very domestic and contented. It's hard to believe that just a few months ago Morris Melgrove was in our lives. Okay, I shouldn't have tried to find Mum a mail-order boyfriend. How was I to know Morris was living on a prison farm, where he was serving time for marrying and marrying without bothering to get a divorce? My intentions were excellent. Anyway, he's back on the prison farm now, growing cabbages. Phew!

'Mum,' I call out. 'Got any ideas about how I can get a job?'

Later, while the three of us sit in the kitchen over dinner, Joe says, 'Well, Hatty, have a look in the local paper. Maybe you can get a job baby-sitting.'

'Or maybe the cake shop down the road needs help over the weekend,' says Mum, thoughtfully.

'Give us a toothpick, love,' says Joe, to

Mum. Mum hands him a small container of toothpicks. I look at his teeth. Little bits of satay chicken splatter the insides of his teeth like graffiti. Joe picks them carefully. I hope he doesn't crack his knuckles in between picking because I will start to scream.

'It's a good idea for you to save for your future, Hatty,' says Mum. 'I don't know about you travelling with Raymond, though. It's too far ahead, but saving is fine.'

Joe finishes his picking. 'Yes,' he says, 'and for every dollar you've saved by the time you're eighteen, Hatty, by golly, I'll match it!'

'Joe,' I say, feeling quite touched, 'that's very generous of you.'

Joe leans his head to one side and smiles. He's a good guy really. The corners of his mouth lift up into swirls of happy wrinkles. Then, he starts to crack his knuckles. The kettle whistles. My nerves shriek. The telephone rings. Saved.

I jump up and rush to the phone. It's Suzy.

Suzy's my best friend, though we're very different. I'm into jazz, she's into grunge. I don't care about being ever-so-slightly tubby and I can't remember the last time I weighed myself. Suzy weighs herself every day and the moment her weight moves up more than half a kilo she goes on a dieting frenzy.

'Hi, Hatty. Wanted to check on the gig

tomorrow. What time is Raymond on?'

'Two o'clock,' I say. Suzy's great that way. She'll come with her boyfriend, Giles, to watch Raymond play, even though they don't really like jazz. We arrange to meet in the garden of the hotel in the afternoon.

When I get off the phone, I rummage around in the lounge room and find the local paper. I look through it carefully but can't find one job I can apply for. There are no baby-sitting jobs and no one is advertising for casual sales assistants. How can I find work?

I flick through the pages and, in a random way, begin to read some of the articles. The mayor has gone off to France to study architecture. Big deal! The local library has bought three new computers. Big deal! Mr Arthur Grainger, solid citizen, former owner of the Glendale Art Studio, has passed away, aged eighty-four. Big deal! Then, I glance through a medical column written by some doctor. People write in with some truly revolting complaints.

'I have a boil on my backside. It just won't go away, no matter what I put on it.' Signed, Martha.

The kind doctor suggests an ointment that is just right for stubborn boils. Big deal! Now me, I'd just tell Martha to pop it and not sit down for a week.

I yawn, as fragments of ideas run through my mind. I could try to get a stall at the local markets. But what could I sell? Maybe I should approach the cake shop down the road. But I might have a compulsive tendency to nibble the cakes. I look again at the newspaper.

'I suffer from indigestion. Nothing stops me burping. What do you suggest?'

The kind doctor suggests a reliable antacid medication. How boring. I'd say something witty like, 'Hold your breath for ten minutes and you'll never suffer from indigestion again.'

I start to think. What if ... what if? No, it wouldn't work. Well, it's a possibility. No. Worth a shot. No. What would Aunt Harriet say? Can't ask her. Joe's talking to Mum in the kitchen. Anyway, the newspaper office probably isn't open today. I'll call on Monday. I'll put it to them. My big idea. My brilliant way to get readers involved with their newspaper. My new job!

Sunday, and we're sitting at a round white table in the Watsons Bay Hotel garden, under a large red umbrella, eating fish and chips. Giles, Suzy and me. Giles is saying, 'Hatty, you're going to turn into a whale if you don't stop eating.'

'Be quiet, Giles Conrad or I'll punch you on the nose.'

It doesn't bother Raymond that I'm slightly overweight. He says I'm a real bargain. He gets more of me to cuddle. And I reckon as long as I can fit into my clothing without serious breathing difficulties I'm okay. Then again, I have bright eyes, clear skin some of the time, full glowing cheeks, silky hair and healthy gaps in my teeth.

Suzy nibbles delicately at her chips and sips her lemonade. Suzy has long fair hair and Giles is what Superman would look like if he was sixteen years old. Lots of muscles, tall with a stubborn chin, darting eyes and a Colgate smile. But he gets sarcastic at times. He doesn't have Raymond's sensitive soul.

The band is really swinging. I'm eating chips with one hand and tapping the table with the other. Giles is staring around at the crowd.

'Reckon Raymond should be pleased. There are a lot of people here. Still, I'm only here because I'm his mate. I like grunge. This stuff is off.'

How could anyone not love jazz? How could anyone not be touched by Raymond's hands moving like sizzling sausages up and down the piano?

I tell Suzy and Giles my idea for getting a job. 'Hatty, that sounds stupid. It'd be a disaster. Have you forgotten what happened the last time you had a loony idea?' asks Giles.

Giles is being very petty in bringing up my good-hearted attempts to match-make my mother. Trust him. Sometimes I almost think he doesn't like me, but Suzy assures me it's not that. He just finds me a bit weird.

I glare at him and feel myself getting hot, and probably turning purple. Suzy gives him a shove with her elbow. He adds hurriedly, 'Don't get me wrong, Hatty, I know you're ambitious, but you couldn't pull this off.'

Suzy wipes her mouth with a paper serviette. 'Give it a go, Hatty. You never know. You're very persuasive. You might talk them into it. What does Raymond think of it?'

I screw up my nose as I remember Raymond's reaction.

'It sounds over the top,' he'd said. 'Maybe you should just wait for a baby-sitting job to come up.'

But he's wrong. They're all wrong. It's really an excellent idea.

The band finishes and everyone claps. I call out, 'More!' Raymond winks at me and the band begins to play 'Sweet Georgia Brown'. I want to get up there and then, and dance. 'Sweet Georgia Brown' does that to me. I really want to swing. I would too, if Giles and Suzy had the guts to join me. But they prefer to go to parties and thrash around to silverchair. I once went to see them with Suzy, and my eardrums took a week to recover. There's no way they'd get high on jazz and I can't see myself dancing alone. So I sit there and savour the music. Let it settle in me.

This is a top day. Watsons Bay with the harbour as a backdrop, and small boats wobbling on water that looks like chopped blue jelly.

Jazz on a summer afternoon. What could be better?

Chapter Two

'So you see, Mr Bates, your newspaper could definitely benefit from an advice column for teenagers. And who could run it better than a teenager?'

It was not easy to get to see Mr Bates, Chief Editor of the *Eastern News*. I'd rung again and again, telling him I had an offer to make him that he couldn't refuse.

'I'm a very busy person, young lady,' he said to me. 'And I can't think of any offer you could make me that I couldn't refuse. Goodbye.'

But when I mentioned my frustration to Joe, he said, 'Old Batesy from the *Eastern News*? Went to school with him. He used to copy my homework. He owes me a favour, by jingo.'

That was how I got Mr Bates to actually listen to my idea on the phone. Then he asked me to send him samples of my writing. The kind of writing I'd use if he agreed to have my column, though, he hastily added, he probably wouldn't.

So I created some very cool questions and answers, faxed them to Mr Bates, and rang him the next day.

'You're very persistent,' he said to me. 'Well, I've read your work, Hatty. It's not bad, not bad at all. Maybe you can come here and we'll have a talk. No promises though.'

Now, Mr Bates, top dog at the *Eastern News*, peers at me from across his desk. His grey hair is combed carefully across a balding scalp. Small glasses sit like twin moons on his nose. His eyes are pale blue and doubtful. He rests his thin head on his thin hand while he studies me.

Still in my school uniform, I sit with my hands clasped together, mature and serious-faced, putting a proposal to Mr Bates.

'Hatty,' he says to me, eventually. 'Let's say I allow you to run an advice column for teenagers. That's quite a responsibility. Could you handle it?'

'No worries,' I tell him. 'I'm an extremely experienced person. I can handle anything, from runaway zits to heavy depression. I've been through it all.'

Mr Bates strokes his chin. He taps a pencil on his desk while he thinks.

'It's not a bad idea,' he says, finally. 'Our medical column is doing very well. Hmm. A teenagers' advice column. We could call it 'Hatty's Hotline' and give it a go for, say, a month. Mind you, I expect you to be totally professional, Hatty. You'll have to call into the office weekly to collect the mail that comes in and be careful to meet our printing deadline. Do you have a computer at home?'

'Sure,' I say, very grateful that, in addition to his mum, Joe brought a computer into the marriage.

'Well, you'll have to type out both the questions and your answers, and you'll need to get the copy back to us on Wednesday afternoon, each week. I owe old Joe a favour.' He leans back in his armchair. 'Who knows, if I hadn't copied his homework, I might never have become a newspaper editor. Ha, ha.'

Suddenly, my head starts to spin like an out-of-control frisbee as reality hits me. I jump up from my seat and run straight at Mr Bates. He looks startled. I think he thinks I'm going to kiss him. It's just that I'm so excited.

'So you're saying I've got the job,' I say, and I grab his hand and shake it hard.

'Hold on, Hatty, and give me my hand back, thank you very much. You're cutting off the circulation. At this stage you've only got a temporary job. We'll pay you, um, fifty dollars a week. Let's say we publish five letters, initially. We'll see how it goes for a month.'

'Mr Bates,' I say, 'you won't be sorry.'

'I'll put an article in the paper this week saying we're starting Hatty's Hotline, an advice column for teenagers,' says Mr Bates. 'When the letters roll in, and that probably won't take long, you can get started.' He smiles at me. 'You're a very persuasive young lady, Hatty. Have you ever thought of going into politics?'

It's hard to wipe the grin off my face when I arrive home. In between peeling vegetables for dinner, I manage to phone Raymond and Suzy. Raymond is amazed.

'You did it! Hatty's Hotline! Wow! It may be hot but it's also very cool, Hatty.'

'Very funny, Raymond.'

I beam. My Raymond, number one kisser, jazz pianist extraordinaire, is definitely proud of me. I phone Suzy next. She squeals, 'Hatty's Hotline! This is too much. You're a genius! Hey, I've got all kinds of problems. I'm going to write a letter to your column this very minute. Wait till I tell Giles.'

Mum and Joe are off their brains with joy. Joe shakes his head and says, 'Well, I never Hatty. You've certainly got what it takes, and old Batesy has shown very good taste.'

Mum puts an arm around me and says, 'My daughter. Only fourteen and having her own newspaper column. I'm so happy.'

Kathryn drops by. Joe is falling over himself with pride.

'Mum,' he says. 'Hatty's got her own newspaper column. She's writing a teenagers' help column for the local paper. Isn't that bonza?'

'Well, I never,' says Kathryn, and her little pale eyes glitter. 'You must take after me, though I can't see how that's possible. I had a column when I was younger. In *Women's Own*. It was a cookery column called "Kitty's Korner". Korner spelt with a 'K'. Kitty's what all my friends called me at school.'

I'm in such a good mood that I forget that Kathryn normally irritates me. I feel very charitable. 'Well, I'll call you Kitty from now on,' I say, and Kitty smiles, but then she gets this strange, doubtful look on her face. Oh well, I'll think about that later. Right now, this is a top day. Mum rings Aunty Sandra who says I am very smart and must take after her. I even get the chance to have a quick talk to Aunt Harriet and her boyfriend, when no one's around.

'I'll make a huge success of this,' I tell Aunt Harriet. 'You wait and see. You made it big in nursing. I'm going to hit the big time in the newspaper world.' In the photograph Harriet gazes lovingly at Thomas, but hey, for a moment I could swear her head turns and her bright eyes flash with pride.

'What do you reckon, Thomas? Do you think I'm going to be a huge success?'

He turns and winks at me. Well – okay – so I've got a vivid imagination.

'Hatty, I thought you'd stopped talking to that photograph?'

It's Mum. She wags a finger at me. I quickly go back to checking the state of the over-boiled vegetables. Kitty walks into the kitchen and glances up at Aunt Harriet.

'Strong chin,' she says. Mum just looks at the two of us and sighs.

I am a real celebrity at school. It's hard to concentrate on Maths, History and English when you're about to have your own newspaper column. Modestly, I don't talk about it, well, not often, but when you have a friend like Suzy you don't have to worry about things like that. By recess, everyone and their dog knows about my column.

Even Suzy's painful little brother Weasel rings me at home. 'Fatty Hatty, I reckon you're doing a good thing for the world. I need advice. I think my teacher smells. How do you reckon I should go about telling him?'

'Weasel,' I say, in my most professional voice, 'honesty is the best policy. Tell your

teacher that there is a vile odour coming from
him, then leave town in a hurry, and
immediately head for the Simpson Desert
without a water bottle and sunhat.'

On Saturday morning, the newspaper prints
a small article inviting young people to write
in with their problems. Hatty from Hatty's
Hotline, teenage guru, will answer all their
worries. I feel very important.

Will I really get a lot of letters? Are there
thousands of maladjusted kids out there, just
begging for my help? Can this be the start of
something big?

It's Tuesday afternoon. I've just been sampling
the chocolate mousse Joe made last night.
He's a very good cook. Kitty's obviously taught
him everything she knows about cooking. The
phone rings. Licking mousse off my fingers, I
rush to it. It's Mr Bates.

'Phew, Hatty,' he says. 'You'd better get
down here. There must be an awful lot of kids
out there with problems. We've got at least
thirty letters for you.'

'I'm not at all surprised, Mr Bates,' I tell him,
trying to sound very cool, when in fact my
heart's drumming furiously. 'You have to
understand that kids need another kid to
confide in.'

I start to rave, but Mr Bates cuts me short.

'Sure, Hatty, listen – can you stop talking and just get down here? Your mail's cluttering up our filing cabinet.'

Joe arrives home from his accounting firm early that day. I beg a lift from him.

'No worries, Hatty,' says Joe. 'Jeepers creepers. Thirty letters. Hatty, you'll become a star. A regular Dorothy Dix. Do you know who she was? She had this advice column in the USA. She was famous.'

Joe's lower jaw twitches with pride. We get in the car and off we go. Joe's a very considerate driver. If he sees people hesitating on the sidewalk doing up their shoelaces, he slows down in case they want to cross the road. He gives way to cars coming in all directions. He even pauses at green lights.

'You can't be too sure,' he tells me, when I start to mutter for him to hurry up. 'I read somewhere that about ten per cent of the population are colour blind so, that being the case, you've got to be extra careful at the lights. You just never know the state of the person's eyes coming in the opposite direction.'

I fidget, and say unkind things in my head about Joe. Eventually, we arrive at the local newspaper. It's a small building squeezed between a supermarket and a florist. I hop out of the car while Joe is deciding whether there is room to park in a spot big enough for two elephants and their offspring.

'Hey, Hatty, don't leap out of the car like that, it's dangerous,' Joe yells at me, looking very annoyed. But I'm in a rush. Got to get my mail. Got to answer all those confused teenagers out there.

I run up to the main desk. Simone, the receptionist, is sitting behind a long desk talking on the phone.

'Yes. No. I can't really say. I've got to give it some thought.'

She waves at me, showing two rows of shiny teeth. I stand there fidgeting. I could barge right past her and make straight for Mr Bates's office but I guess I'd better be polite. Maybe she's talking to the mayor or the Prime Minister or somebody like that.

'Getting my eyelashes tinted is a big decision,' she says, wriggling the telephone cord. I give her a very pained frown. 'Uh oh, better go, duty calls.'

'Hatty.' She beams at me as she puts the telephone down. 'You're a very popular girl. I've got your mail right here.'

Simone stands up. She's wearing a short navy suit and has legs that most girls would die for. She goes to a grey metal cupboard against the wall, opens it up and pulls out a bulging plastic bag.

'Letters,' says Simone. 'Heaps of them.'

At that moment, Joe walks in. 'Good grief, Hatty,' he says, when he sees Simone hand me the bag of mail. 'If this continues we'll have to rent a truck.' Just then, Mr Bates comes out to the reception desk. He and Joe shake hands.

'Remember when you won the burping contest at school?' asks Joe. 'And the time you mixed the wrong stuff together in science and blew up the lab?'

Simone starts to laugh.

'Ahem, nice to see you again, Joe. Whoops, there goes my phone.' Mr Bates gives us all a sick smile, as he hurries out of the room.

'He was a great burper,' comments Joe.

I look at my bag of mail. This is very good. This is wonderful. I am a success. Now, all I have to do is find a way to cope with my English homework, find time to go to the park with Raymond, because the tree planting program has begun (and you know what that means), and answer my adoring fans.

On the way home, Joe's mum flashes through my brain. She had a column too. Kitty's Korner by Kitty Litta. That's when the penny drops. Kitty Litter. No wonder she got that strained look on her face when I said I'd call her Kitty. Kitty Litter. What a gas! Uh oh, my bladder's bursting. I don't think I'm going to make it home. Think deserts. Think sand dunes and barren landscapes. On no account think of running taps. Joe, drive a bit quicker. Please don't give way to that paper bag. Kitty Litter. It's too much.

Chapter Three

Mum turns on the mother act when I get home and says I can't even look, not even peek, at my letters until I've finished my homework. How boring! I write my English essay. I fiddle around with my Maths homework. I study History. At half-past seven, when Mum and Joe are sitting talking in the lounge room, I finally pour all those precious letters out of the plastic bag onto my bed. Letters in long envelopes, letters in short envelopes. My name. MY NAME on the outside. Hatty's Hotline, the *Eastern News*. I feel very proud. Hatty's Hotline. I say it over and over to myself.

I grab a letter, any letter, and prise open the envelope. A folded typewritten page is inside. I read:

Dear Hatty,

I am really glad that there is a column in

the paper for teenagers like me with terrible problems.

I have two boyfriends. They don't know about each other and I can't make up my mind which one I like best. They are both good-looking with great personalities. The trouble is, if they find out that I'm two-timing them, I'll probably lose them both. How can I make a decision about which one to keep and which one to drop?

Good luck with your new column,

Carla

P.S. Please publish this letter. It would be so cool to see it in print.

This is an extremely serious problem. How can this be compared to Martha, who wrote in to the doctor for advice about boils on her backside? What incredible advice can I give Carla? How to solve the dilemma of the two gorgeous guys.

The phone rings. Mum calls out, 'Hatty, it's for you. It's Suzy.'

Usually, Suzy and I talk on the phone forever, but now her timing is bad. I run into the lounge room, pick up the phone and tell her I've collected my mail from the newspaper office.

'Well,' she says. 'What's in the letters? Quick, tell me.'

I become defensive. 'I've only read one and I can't discuss it, Suzy. Now, don't scream at me. You've got to understand, it's all private. I'm a lifeline for some of these kids. Without me, well, they might need serious therapy.'

'*You're* going to need serious therapy if you don't share this with me, Hatty Duncan. I mean, what are best friends for?'

I try to stick to my principles. 'I've only read one whole letter, and it was just the usual boyfriend stuff. I'm a teenage shrink now and it's all very confidential. But, if anything really out of the ordinary comes up, like say, a teenager with an uncontrollable urge to bungee jump from the Harbour Bridge, honest, you'll be the first to know.'

'Hmm,' says Suzy. 'Well, things are boring around here, and Weasel's driving me crazy, so I'm relying on your column to add some spice to my life.'

After I get off the phone I go back to my bedroom. I sit on my bed and thumb quickly through different letters.

Dear Hatty,

I don't get on with my mother or father.

They're too strict. They won't even let me catch a bus to the city by myself. I feel stupid because all my friends have so much more freedom than me. What can I do?'

Tamie

That's an enormous problem, Tamie. I've got to give that intense thought.

Mum comes into my bedroom, carrying a glass of strawberry soda. 'How's it going?' she asks me. She sits on the chair by the bed and smiles at the stack of letters.

'Mum,' I say, 'they're only going to publish five letters a week. What about all these other letters? What if this small hill of letters turns into a Mount Everest? I've got to answer all these kids. They're relying on me. The stamps alone will cost me a fortune.'

'Take it easy, Hatty,' says Mum, and she passes me the glass of strawberry soda, which I down in one thirsty gulp. 'If you want to answer all those letters, ask the newspaper to tell your writers to send in a stamped self-addressed envelope. I don't know how you're going to find the time to answer everyone personally, though.'

Joe wanders into my room. 'I'm impressed, Hatty. You've shown real initiative in getting this job.'

'And you know what, Joe,' I tell him, happily. 'In three and a half years, when I'm eighteen, if my column is still going, I'll have over seven thousand dollars. That makes fourteen thousand if you match it dollar for dollar, like you promised.'

Joe turns pale and walks out of the room, muttering to himself.

Mum curls up on the end of my bed. She hugs a cushion then puts it absently to one side, looking troubled.

'What's up, Mum? It's Kitty Litter, isn't it? And don't say it isn't because your nostrils have begun to flare.'

'Hatty . . .' Mum says. 'Don't call her that. She's a, well, a nice old lady. I like her.'

'Mum, have you forgotten who you're talking to? I'm Hatty from Hatty's Hotline. Super teen guru. I KNOW these things. You've just got to talk to Joe. Tell him you need space. You can't have Kitty Litter coming over every day. I like her too, well, some of the time. But, honestly, we've got no privacy. Also, while you're talking to Joe about his mum, do you think you could mention his knuckles? And maybe the way he picks food out of his teeth? It's not that I don't have obnoxious habits . . .'

'Hatty, ease up,' says Mum. She twists her hands in her lap and her nostrils flare like two open trumpets, as she says, 'I really don't mind Kitty, um Kathryn, coming over all the time. Well, maybe a bit.' I watch, fascinated, as her dilated nostrils slacken. 'I'd just like a bit more time with Joe and you.'

'I know, Mum.' I reach into my pocket. 'Here, have a Malteser. You'll feel better.'

Later that week, Kitty invites me over to her flat. She's been busy doing it up and she tells me proudly I am the first visitor. I don't really want to go, but Joe and Mum have taken sickies from work so they can be mushy around the house and that sort of thing, and I reckon that as a kind of teen psychologist I should give them time together. Also, Kitty sounded lonely over the phone. So, while Joe and Mum are home slobbering over each other, I go and visit her after school. Kitty's flat is in a neat building of four apartments. The garden is full of leafy shrubs.

Kitty lets me in. She's wearing a pair of baggy trousers and a sleeveless blouse.

'Come in, child,' she says to me. 'Dear me, you've gained weight, haven't you, Hatty?'

'It's Joe's cooking,' I say, defensively.

What's she on about? If my weight doesn't bother me, it shouldn't bother her.

Kitty Litter's place is very neat and personal. Everywhere there are touches that say, 'Hey, Kitty Litter lives here'. She has small paintings of flowers on the hall wall, and ornamental gnomes on a little coffee table. Everything is arranged just so.

She proudly shows me her bedroom. There's a small bed, a wardrobe and a dressing-table with a flowered doily and two brightly coloured gnomes sitting on it. It is exceptionally gross.

'It looks great,' I say, hoping she's not telepathic.

Then we go through to the lounge room. She definitely has a thing about gnomes and the colour yellow. She has four bright yellow armchairs with yellow cushions on them, and on the polished floor she has a yellow rug with daisies embroidered on it. Yellow curtains complete the picture. My feeling on entering the room is of finding myself in the desert without a pair of sunglasses to cut the glare.

From here we go into a little kitchen. It's just a regular, normal kitchen with neat little tiles on the floor and a white fridge with all kinds of daggy magnets holding up pictures. There's one of me there, squinting at the camera on Mum and Joe's wedding day. And there's a photo of Kitty Litter with Mum and Joe.

On the wall are some framed black and white photographs of people in old-fashioned clothing. A white-haired lady sits on a chair with a stern-looking man standing beside her.

Kitty sees me staring at the photo. 'My parents,' she says. 'Joe's grandparents. Your step great-grandparents, I suppose, Hatty.'

'Your parents,' I repeat. 'Wow! They look so, I don't know, serious, Kitty. Didn't people smile then?'

'That's just the pose, Hatty,' says Kitty. 'Then again, maybe they'd just come back from the dentist. Now, sit down and I'll dish you up some of my meat loaf. It tastes so good you'll want to move in with me, Hatty.'

Kitty Litter smiles. I don't.

Raymond is one class ahead of me at school. We're both pretty busy now. He's got heaps of homework and then there's gig practice with his group. I've got heaps of homework and then there's my column.

I have to select five letters from those I've received. Five to be published. I go through all the letters carefully. Eventually, I come up with five really different problems. The boy with zits who can't get a girl to go out with him. The girl whose parents are too strict. A few girl/boy, boy/girl problems.

I type out the letters to be published on the computer. Then I think and think. I eat and think. I make a milkshake for myself and think. I make myself a large toasted cheese sandwich and think. Eventually my well-fed brain cells stretch themselves and this is what I come up with:

Dear F (the boy with zits – real name suppressed),

It's rotten to have zits. They get really attached to you even though you don't like them at all. The good news is that sooner or later zits pack their bags, leave home and settle on someone else's tasty skin. While you're waiting for that to happen, try not to squeeze them, no matter how juicy they are, and see a skin specialist.

Cut down on chocolate and greasy food because zits feed on them. Even a tiny zit turns into a mega-zit when confronted with chocolate, because the excitement is too great for it.

Meantime, exercise and develop your muscles, and pooh to all those girls who won't go out with you.

Hatty

There. A brilliant, psychologically sound answer to a mortifying problem.

To Tamie, who needs more freedom, I say:

Dear T,

It's really tough when you feel your parents don't trust you enough to let you get a bus to the city. I suggest you point out to them that they trusted you enough to let you out of nappies when you were younger, and that they trust you not to throw up in public. They also trust you not to pull dogs' tails or to stomp on the neighbour's vegetable patch.

It's time they went that one step further and trusted you to get a bus to the city by yourself. If they still say 'no', get someone they trust to speak to them. Maybe your family doctor could tell them that you might develop nervous habits like bed-wetting if you aren't given more freedom. That should bring them round.

Hatty

There. I am a psychological genius. A teenage shrink wizard.

To Carla with the two gorgeous boyfriends, I write this:

Dear C,

You are very lucky to have not one but two gorgeous guys crazy about you. However, you are swimming in deep water and are about to drown. You've got to let one go or you'll sink quicker than the Titanic. If you can't choose between two equally fantastic guys, toss a coin or play eenie meenie miney mo.

Hatty

To James, who is in love with Amanda, who is in love with Greg:

Give up. Your spaceship has bypassed the moon and is on a collision course with Mars. Accept defeat gracefully. You cannot make someone love you.

You have to find someone who thinks you're irresistible. Meantime, try to get more confidence in yourself. Practise smiling in the mirror saying, "Wow, I'm cute!"

To Meg, who is in love with Paul, who is in love with himself:

Anyone who is so selfish he only takes you to places he enjoys, like football, and who won't let you wear sun-screen down the beach because he says it makes you slippery, is a loser. I'd let him slide right away.

When I have finished typing out my letters I check them, pat myself on my back, check them again, pat myself on my back again, print them out and put the neatly typed pages in a large envelope. Tomorrow after school I'll drop it into the newspaper office.

I nick into the kitchen. Mum and Joe are eating cake and discussing painting the walls pale lavender. I whisper to Aunt Harriet and Thomas.

'I'm fantastic. Just wanted to let you know. And don't worry. I won't let them paint the walls lavender. It will do nothing for your complexion, Aunt Harriet.'

'Hatty,' Mum interrupts. 'I heard that. What is there about that picture that makes you talk to it?'

'Everyone's got their odd habits,' I say defensively, just as Joe begins to crack his knuckles.

Chapter Four

I AM THE GREATEST! No two ways about it. My column takes off like an Oasis concert. There I am in print, with MY name, Hatty's Hotline, spread across the top of a whole half page, followed by letters from confused teenagers and MY slick, sensible answers. Mr Bates is pleased. Aunt Harriet and Thomas are pleased. Mum and Joe are pleased. Kitty Litter is also pleased.

'By crikey, you're definitely on the road to success,' says Joe, as he studies my column. 'I've married into a famous family.'

'Shucks, Joe,' I say humbly.

'Without a doubt, Hatty, I see a bright sparkling future for you,' says Kitty.

'That's because she's such a bright spark,' says Joe, and everyone cracks up at his brilliant joke.

The letters roll in like high tide on Bondi Beach. It's amazing the number of troubled kids out there all needing help from Hatty's Hotline.

Raymond comes over after school one day while I'm sitting at my desk chewing the end of my pen. I take him into the kitchen and open two cans of Coke.

He studies the picture of Aunt Harriet and Thomas. 'Your aunt must have seen some rotten things in Europe just after the war. Do you know you look a bit like her?'

'Hello, Hatty. Hello, Raymond.' It's Kitty Litter. She's suddenly there in the kitchen, as irritating as chicken pox. 'Heard what you said about Harriet. Yes, Hatty does look a little like her. They have the same clear eyes and firm chin. She must have been some woman.'

'She was,' I say proudly, but I'm a bit miffed. I need time alone with Raymond.

And then, would you believe it, Kitty plonks herself next to Raymond and the two of them start to talk about jazz. That's MY scene, not Kitty's. I slurp on my Coke, stare up at Aunt Harriet and Thomas, and send them dark thought messages about how it's time for Kitty Litter to go home.

I fidget and tap my fingers a few hundred times, but Raymond and Kitty are in deep conversation. Eventually, I say, 'Maybe I'll get back to my column. You two don't seem to need me around.'

'Cut it out, Hatty,' says Raymond. He has a curly frown on his forehead. 'You're so touchy nowadays.'

'Well, you're so deep in conversation, you obviously don't need me around.'

'Actually I thought we might walk to the park.' Raymond winks at me. 'The tree planting's begun.'

'The three of us could go together,' says Kitty.

'Uum . . .' says Raymond. Go on, Raymond. Finish the sentence. Tell Kitty Litter that the park is OUR park. When we do go, it's just the two of us. There are about a hundred newly planted trees there and we've made this pact, see, to have meaningful kisses beside each tree. Tell her, Raymond.

'Ah, well actually . . .' says Raymond, and he studies the magnets on the fridge.

Is this my Raymond? My hero! He's turning into a prize wimp.

'I've got to work anyway,' I say abruptly. 'You'd better go.'

Raymond gets up from his chair, looking annoyed. Kitty waves a cheery goodbye to him. 'What's with you, Hatty?' Raymond asks, as I follow him up the hall.

'I'm busy,' I say. 'And we don't get much time together and when you come over she's here. And you ignored me and encouraged her.'

42

I open the front door for him, feeling very miffed. He hesitates, looking a bit confused, then leans across and kisses me. A soft gentle, 'Hey, it's me' kiss on the lips. 'Take it easy, Hatty. You're overdoing this Hotline thing. Think of all those new trees in the park.'

I stare into his magnificent, brilliant, inspiring, dreamy, wonderful, expressive, dark eyes. I'm nuts. He's not really a wimp. He's just sensitive, caring, considerate and cute.

I give him a meaningful kiss back, and after he goes I lean against the front door, daydreaming. Raymond and I on a desert island. No one else but the two of us and a coconut tree. Raymond and I on a raft, drifting across the Pacific Ocean to South America. Just the two of us, Coca Cola and a carton of Maltesers.

'Do you want help with your letters, Hatty? I've got a bit of spare time if you need me,' Kitty calls out.

A small fuse in me explodes. 'I don't need your help. It's MY column.' I run to my bedroom and bang my door shut. Good thing that Mum and Joe aren't home. They'd go ballistic.

I sit at my desk and pull out the week's letters. I hear the front door quietly click open then close. Then the patter of shoes and the creak of the front gate. Kitty Litter's gone home. Good! So why is my stomach a guilty mass of tangled rope?

I read my letters.

Dear Hatty,

For the past two weeks I have been having the most terrible nightmares. I keep dreaming that I am a vampire and that I am breaking into homes sucking blood out of teenage girls' necks. How can I stop these terrible dreams?

Henry

Hmm. Obviously, a dud letter from a smart alec.

Dear Henry,

If the nightmares continue, be a considerate vampire and carry bandaids for your victims. Meantime, file your teeth.

Hatty

Here's a serious one.

Dear Hatty,

How do I go about talking to boys? I go to an all-girls school. I don't have brothers, or even boy cousins, so my contact with boys is zilch. When I get to speak to boys my lips go numb, my heart bangs and my stomach rumbles. I am quite sure that everyone can hear my heart pounding and my stomach rumbling and it's very embarrassing. What can I do?

Signed,
Sharon

Hmm. Hmm. Hmm. It's hard to put myself in Sharon's place. I've never been shy with boys and, what's more, I don't have any brothers or boy cousins. Boys. What's to be scared of?

Dear Sharon,

It's sad that your lips go numb, your heart bangs and your stomach rumbles, all on account of you trying to make an impression on boys.

Firstly, don't worry about your heart banging; no one can hear it and it's a

45

healthy sign that you're alive. If your lips go numb, give them a quick sharp bite. That's bound to bring the feeling back. As for your stomach rumbling. Make sure there's lots of food in it when encountering a boy. That way your stomach is so busy digesting grub it doesn't have time to make noises.

On a practical note, you've got to get off your butt and join a club where there are BOYS as well as girls. Be brave. Remember that even Superman started out as mild-mannered Clark Kent.

Hatty

Yet another brilliant answer to a complex problem. Let's look at the next one.

Dear Hatty,

I have a friend. She's just started a teenage advice column in the newspaper. I have noticed lately that she has trouble getting around on account of the size of her head. What do you suggest I do?

Signed,
Someone You Know Very Well

I write personally back to Suzy on that one.

Dear S,

Everyone has a special moment in their life when all the stars are in alignment, when the great wheels of the universe turn in their direction. This is known to result in a temporary increase in the size of the head. Be understanding. This is your friend's great moment in time.

Hatty

PS. I'll phone you soon – promise.

My days are busy. There's school, and trying to keep up with homework. There are the endless questions from school friends about the column, and honestly, I try to be modest, but it's hard at times. Suddenly, I'm a somebody, and troubled kids I hardly know come to me for advice on all sorts of things.

Then, there's Raymond, and I've got to be supportive and go along to gigs at the weekend and clap like mad and stomp my feet. But now I take along a notebook and pen and I dash off answers to my letters ready to type up on the computer when I get home.

'I've got one hundred and fifty dollars in the bank,' I tell Raymond proudly. We're in the garden of the Watsons Bay Hotel and he's having a break from playing. The sun is hot, the sky is blue and Raymond is squinting at his lemon squash, while his dad has a beer with the other members of the band.

'You don't seem to have much time for me nowadays,' Raymond comments. 'You seem obsessed with your column.'

I'm offended. 'Raymond, this is for us. The only reason I'm writing the column is because it gives me a way to put money aside.' Major lie. I am having the time of my life. I have never felt so important. 'I come to your gigs.'

'But you were sitting there writing in your notebook right through "Sweet Georgia Brown",' complains Raymond. 'I thought that was our song.'

I squirm. Can't believe that. I WROTE in my notebook while 'Sweet Georgia Brown' was on. 'I was listening. Honest. You were terrific.'

Raymond frowns. He taps the table absently with his fingers, finishes his drink and goes quiet. I hate that. Why can't he just be totally unreasonable and rant and rave?

I put my notebook away in my bag. He notices and a smile flickers on his face. 'Good,' he says. 'Forget about your Hotline for now. This is my gig.'

He winks at me and joins the rest of the band. His hands slide over the piano. The music goes on and on. I sit, nervously clutching my hands under the table, a fixed, tortured smile on my face, as Raymond turns his head from time to time and grins at me. I've got all these letters to answer. Why is he so edgy? Doesn't he understand? Doesn't anyone understand?

'We've only been speaking for three-quarters of an hour. What's the rush?' (Suzy, Tuesday night, 8.30 pm. I still haven't finished my column and the deadline is, oh no, tomorrow afternoon.)

'Hatty, you've got to help in the house. I'm working, Joe's working and you've got to pull your weight.' (Mum, discovering an ant colony around the sink after I was supposed to clean up.)

'Come on, Hatty, let's have a bit of family spirit. Crikey, I thought you were a Star Trek fan. Come and sit with us and we can all beam up together. Ha ha.' (Joe, jaw twitching, picking popcorn out of his teeth in front of the TV).

'Hatty, when are you going to come and visit me again?' (Kitty Litter, apparently recovered from my outburst.)

'You two are the only ones who keep quiet and let me get on with the job,' I mutter to Aunt Harriet and Thomas.

Chapter Five

'He's going to look just fine in your front garden,' says Kitty Litter to Mum. Kitty is holding a chubby-faced ceramic garden gnome. He's about half the size of my school ruler, has a red peaked hat, a white beard, bushy white eyebrows, an orange shirt and green trousers. He holds a miniature garden rake and stares at us with a cheeky smile on his face. In a word he's GROSS.

Mum glances hopefully at Joe for support. 'I'm sure it's very nice,' she says, and her nostrils blow up like two inflatable rafts. Joe takes the gnome from Kitty and says, 'By golly, Mum, he's just so cute. This knocks me out. Reminds me of when I was a kid. Remember all the garden gnomes we had in the garden? I used to call them gernomees. Ha, ha.'

Kitty puts her skinny hands on her skinny hips, throws back her head and laughs. Joe, clutching the gernomee, laughs too. Mum and I exchange quick, worried looks.

'Where are we going to put it, Mum?' I ask.

'I think it will be um, quite happy, near the hydrangeas,' says Mum. Then, she forces a brave smile. 'Thanks, Kitty. It's very kind of you.'

'Love garden gnomes myself,' says Kitty. 'When I was a kid I used to talk to them. At times they seemed to make a lot more sense than my friends.'

The placing of the gnome in the front garden is done with ceremony. Mum wants him to be half-hidden by the hydrangeas, which have a way of drooping, and might therefore render the gernomee invisible. Joe and Kitty want to put him next to the carnations.

'Ron has a better view from there,' says Kitty.

'Ron?' Mum and I say, together.

'You've got to name them,' Kitty says to us. 'This one's called Ron.'

So, Ron is stuck between a yellow and a red carnation. Mum winces as Joe places him gently on the earth. 'There you go, Ron,' he says.

We walk back into the house. Joe washes his hands in the bathroom and whistles to himself.

I put on the kettle while Mum takes some cups and saucers from the drainer near the sink. She fumbles around, opening a side cupboard.

'Where are my tea towels? Surely, we haven't run out.'

'You've got plenty, Margaret,' says Kitty. 'But I thought they looked happier in the linen cupboard next to the sheets.'

'Happier? How can tea towels look happier?'

'If you like, I'll put them back where they were. I was only trying to be helpful.' Kitty's face turns into a wriggly mass of worry lines.

'No, it's okay,' says Mum. She bites her lip.

I disappear into my bedroom and shut the door quickly. Kitty Litter should get herself a life. She could go walking on the beach. She could bake cookies for hospitals or buy herself a cat and then she'd be Kitty Litter buying Kitty Litter for her Kitty. Ha, ha.

I concentrate on my English homework. The tragedy of Macbeth. The tragedy right now is that I don't seem to have time to do my homework. I chew the end of my pen. Kitty has such a loud voice. Could that be Mum and Kitty arguing? There goes the door and it's being banged shut. Ah, finally, peace, glorious peace. Back to Macbeth.

'She's MY mum.' Now it's Joe, having a scream. Keep your voice down, Joe, or I'll have to buy ear plugs, and I heard of one getting lost down an ear-drum and being coughed up two months later.

'We've got to have a bit of privacy. Do you

know, Joe, she's even put all the books in alphabetical order on the shelves! Why'd she do that? And she's bought more yellow cushions for the sofa.'

Good on you, Mum. Go for it. The voices become softer. I hear the heavy tread of shoes along the hall. A door quietly opens and closes. A car engine starts. Then, there is a stillness in the house. Not even the whirr of a lawn-mower or the tick of a clock. Back to Macbeth.

Later, when I've finished my homework, I stand up, stretch, yawn and come out to get something to eat. I find that I have Mum all to myself. Joe's gone out and she's sitting on the sofa in the lounge room, with a finger in her mouth.

'What's for dinner?' I ask.

'Can't you think about anything except your column and food?'

'What's up? Where's Joe? No, don't say that he's gone to buy milk. Just tell me that he's taken Kitty to the North Pole and she won't be back until she's built herself an igloo.'

Suddenly, without breaking into hives, which usually happens when she's going under, Mum starts to cry. Her shoulders heave as tears roll down her cheeks like mini boulders.

I rush to her and sit behind her, awkwardly

trying to hug her, but she pushes me away.

'You're not very helpful, Hatty. No one's very helpful. And now that awful gnome. It's not just that I hate garden gnomes. It's what it stands for. It's another way of Kitty taking over the house. I love Joe, even though you may find that hard to understand.'

Mum wags her finger at me as I start to protest. 'Don't try to deny it, Hatty. I can read your face very well. Joe's good-hearted and there for us when we need him. He may not be Richard Gere or Arnold Schwarzenegger but he's my Joe. And we've just had our first . . . our first . . . fight. And he's stormed out. And he's gone running over to Kitty's flat. And all because I suggested very gently to Kitty that she might like to visit us less and take up a hobby.'

'Like maybe mountain climbing without an oxygen mask,' I add. 'Okay, sorry, Mum, I won't try to be funny. I understand. I do. Honest. But surely Joe knows that his first obligation is to you, not his mother?'

'He's never been married before, Hatty. It isn't his fault. He's an only child and his mother means a lot to him. I'm not trying to come between them. I just need more time alone with him.'

I hand Mum some tissues from the coffee table. She blows her nose noisily.

'I reckon you and Joe should get some counselling. I'd help you myself but I'm only good at teen stuff.'

'Hatty, you're impossible,' says Mum, and suddenly the sun comes out as she puts her hand over her mouth and tries not to giggle. 'We'll sort it out, I suppose. Now, get back to your homework or whatever. I want to wash these tears away before Joe comes home.'

While Mum's in the bathroom I quickly nick out to the kitchen to talk to Aunt Harriet and Thomas.

'Things aren't going all that well,' I whisper to them. 'Joe's mum is a royal pain. What do you think we should do?'

Aunt Harriet stares lovingly into Thomas's eyes. I don't think she's listening to me today.

The phone rings. It's Raymond.

'The tree planting's finished,' he tells me, and his voice is rushed and excited. 'Don't make any plans for tomorrow after school.'

He is so cute. 'No way,' I say. Then I remember. 'It's Wednesday. I've got to deliver my copy to the newspaper. We'll have to break our kissing record on Thursday afternoon.'

'I've got to rehearse with the band then.'

'Well, that's not my fault, Raymond. The trees will still be there at the weekend.'

'Can't you drop off your stuff to the

newspaper office on the way to school tomorrow?'

'No, there's no time. Can't you ask the band to rehearse on Friday instead of Thursday afternoon?'

'You know I can't.'

There's an awkward hesitation. Finally, Raymond says stiffly, 'If you got up early tomorrow, I reckon you could manage to drop off the letters at the newspaper office. I'm getting fed up with you, Hatty. You're always putting me off.'

'Oh yeah, well, if you weren't a wimp you'd tell your dad and the rest of the band that it's more important we set a kissing record than rehearse for a dumb gig on Sunday.'

'My gig's not dumb. That's a rotten thing to say.'

'Well, you don't seem to understand how I feel about my column.'

'Yeah?'

'Yeah.'

My forehead feels sweaty. How can he be so insensitive?

'Got to go,' I say abruptly, and I put the phone down.

There's nothing like the sounds of silence in my house to make me feel super-sensitive to any noise at all. I can hear my own jagged breathing. If I listen hard enough I can probably hear the lions roaring at Taronga Park Zoo and that's seventeen kilometres away. Right now, the drop of a pin would sound like a huge avalanche.

Joe comes home and he's extremely quiet. He seems to pad through the house in gloved feet. I help Mum cook dinner and later the three of us sit in an awkward huddle around the kitchen table.

Joe is obviously quite distressed because, despite the fact that the meat is rather stringy, he doesn't pick his teeth once. Mum flicks potato from the side of her mouth and asks me mundane questions about school. Joe's Adam's apple bounces up and down like a yo-yo, as he washes the stringy meat down with water, then asks me mundane questions about school. Joe and Mum throw each other uneasy looks, while the silence between them cuts the air like a big knife.

I glance up at Aunt Harriet. Hey, I say in my mind, do something. We're in big trouble, here.

Eventually, when I can't stand the tension any longer, I say, 'I'm going to the front garden. I might have a word with Ron.'

Joe's lips twitch a bit at that. 'Good idea, Hatty. I might join you later.'

I leave the two of them there, clattering their

knives and forks, and go outside. There's Ron, the garden gernomee, perched between the carnations, a glazed garden rake in his hand, a zany smile on his mouth and two dots for eyes, as he watches the world go by.

I gently hose the garden, watching sunlight turning the water jet into a sparkling rainbow. I'll give Ron a good shower. After all, I wouldn't want him to get smelly armpits in all this heat. When the garden is thoroughly soaked, and Ron is looking as if a ceramic umbrella wouldn't go astray, I turn off the hose, and go back inside.

I hear a giggle followed by a sigh. An 'Oh, Joe . . .' followed by more giggling and Joe saying, 'Margaret, oh Margaret.'

They're back at it. All mush and sloppiness. Phew! I feel kind of relieved.

Raymond hasn't rung back. He will though. He'll see reason. Surely, kissing me comes before a band rehearsal. He'll phone, won't he?

Chapter Six

It's Wednesday afternoon and I've just arrived, out of breath, at the newspaper office. I had to shop for vegetables on the way home from school, then I missed the bus and I thought I'd never make it to the office in time. Mr Bates is standing next to Simone's desk talking to her. They both look up at me as I walk in.

'Got my copy for this week's paper,' I gasp, fumbling through my bags.

'Hello Hatty,' says Mr Bates. He walks out from behind the desk and puts his hand lightly on my shoulder. 'I want a photo of you to put above your column.' He smiles at me. 'We can take one here, or maybe you have a favourite one at home.'

Imagine! My face at the top of my column. I feel squishy inside. This is so cool. I try not to drool with excitement. Got to be professional.

'Also,' says Mr Bates. 'I've decided to give you a full page. Your column is doing quite well. Of course it will mean a bit of extra work for you, but I'll increase your wage.'

'Wow,' I say. I grab Mr Bates's hand and start shaking it. 'Thanks, Mr Bates, you won't be sorry.'

'Hatty, give me back my hand. It's going numb.' Mr Bates pulls his hand away from me and stares at it. 'You've got the grip of a sumo wrestler. Anyway, keep up the good work,' he says, walking away.

A full page. More money. Raymond and I will be able to travel all over the world. We can go trekking in Mongolia and bungee jump over the Grand Canyon. We can . . .

'Wake up, Hatty,' says Simone. She flicks her blonde hair back from her forehead, uncrosses her drop-dead legs and lifts a large plastic bag from beside her desk. She winks at me. 'Here are this week's problems, Hatty. Oh, and my niece wants your autograph.'

Simone produces a kid's autograph book. I proudly write a small greeting on a pale pink page and sign my best Hatty signature.

I have a fan. I have a full page in the *Eastern News*. There'll be a mug shot of me above my column. I'll be famous. Stopped in the street and at supermarkets. I'll have to buy a pair of dark sunglasses. Dye my hair. Even dart into alleyways to avoid being mobbed.

'Hatty, you've got an out-of-body look in

your eyes. Here, take your letters.'

I hand Simone a bag containing my copy for the newspaper, take this week's problems, and, attempting to appear casual and sophisticated, wave goodbye to Simone. I somehow manage to walk to the office door without breaking into an excited run.

'Hey, Hatty,' yells Simone. 'Come back. You've left me a bag full of carrots and potatoes.'

Running a newspaper column is very serious stuff. Apart from the process of selecting the letters that will go in the paper, I try to answer all my mail, and, like Jack's beanstalk, it's growing like mad.

I divide the mail into two lots. The serious letters, like teenagers with enormous girl/boy problems, and the non-urgent stuff, such as how to cope with bus drivers who become abusive when handed last year's bus pass.

I answer all my mail because, hey, I'm Hatty's Hotline. Without me those troubled teenagers would have to turn to their friends or family for advice. Also, I have a well-padded ego that is having a very happy trip with all this fame.

Raymond and I make up over the weekend. I decide to back down and ring him.

'Raymond,' I say. 'I'm sorry if I've been out

of sorts. I didn't mean what I said.' (The truth is I am so tired that I can't remember exactly what I've said to offend Raymond.)

'Hmm,' says Raymond. 'Okay, but don't let it happen again, Hatty.'

'Sure.' I squirm. Surely I haven't been *that* insulting, and anyway, doesn't everyone have their bad days?

But then, there are all those trees at the park and Raymond is a very meaningful kisser.

'We've set some kind of record,' I say to him dreamily, as we walk hand-in-hand through the park. 'Look, Raymond, there's another tree.'

Well, it's hardly a tree, more a tiny plant, but it'll do. I pucker up as Raymond lands a beaut one on my lips.

'We'll be at the Watsons Bay Hotel again on Sunday afternoon. You are coming, aren't you?' he asks, on the way home.

'Sure,' I say. 'Well, I'm almost sure. That is . . .'

'You'll come if you've finished writing your column, is that what you want to say, Hatty?' Raymond kicks angrily at a stray stone.

'Um, well, you see, Raymond, Mr Bates has offered me a full page. A full page in the *Eastern News!* Raymond, don't you understand what that means?'

'It means you'll have no time to see me or come to my gigs.'

'Hey, you should be happy for me. This is a terrific opportunity. Of course I'll come to your gigs. Remember me, I'm your greatest fan.' I try to give Raymond my most appealing Princess Di look, dipping my head and looking up at him from under my lashes.

Raymond doesn't seem impressed. 'Sure I'm glad for you,' he says, in an unenthusiastic voice, 'but you're taking on too much, Hatty. It's got to put pressure on us.'

'No way,' I say. Inside, I mentally bite my nails because there's so much to do. Letters and homework. Homework and letters. Suzy trying to see me, too. And of course, I've got to go to Raymond's gigs. But then, shouldn't he be more understanding?

Later, I sit at my desk in front of the navy-blue face of my computer and read my mail.

Dear Hatty,

My life has come to an end. My boyfriend went overseas with his parents to live in Spain. He may never come back. I miss him so much, and please don't tell me to meet other boys because I've tried that, and it

just doesn't work. Last week he wrote to
tell me that he'd met someone else and I
am in so much pain I really can't cope.
It hurts so much. How can I get on with my
life?

Signed,
Tearful Tessa

Hmm. Deep thought. Food. I definitely need a
Malteser break. My brain cells need extra
nourishment so they don't shrivel. Four
Maltesers and one strawberry soda later, I go
back to the computer.
    Inspiration.

Dear Tearful Tessa,

Unfortunately, you just have to slowly get
on with your life. Cry a bit and let time
pass.
    Think of how you waited and waited for
your boobs to appear and suddenly, when
you'd given up hope, these two perky lumps
suddenly sprouted on your chest.
    Life's like that. Just when you think
nothing's going to happen to make you feel
good, it does.
    Keep busy. Sooner or later someone

special will come into your life again.

Hatty

Hmm. I need at least ten letters for my first full page. Ten really good letters. A mixture of meaningful problems. Let's have a look at this one.

Dear Hatty,

I hope you can help me. Recently, my grandfather came to live with us after my grandmother died. I used to like him but now he's driving me crazy. He criticises everything I do and is generally a big pain.
    The thing is, he's here to stay, so how do I go about getting on with him and staying sane?

Your true fan,
Victor

I sit and think about that one. The grandfather is obviously missing his wife and doesn't know what to do with himself. Poor old guy. He needs an interest. Something or someone to bring the sparkle back into his life. He could take up bowling maybe. Or play cards. Do some gardening. Take up parachute jumping. He needs a hobby. Then again, he might need a lady friend.

Hmm. I need to consider this carefully.

'Yoo hoo. It's me, Kitty.'

I groan as I hear the front door open and Kitty's stomping feet marching down the hall.

Did I mention that everyone at home made up with everyone else? There were kisses and hugs all round. Mum held Kitty Litter to her and said she didn't mean to be insulting by suggesting that she spend less time with them. You should have seen Mum's nostrils inflate when she told that whopper. Then, Joe held Mum to his chest and said she was the best, most understanding wife in the world. Then I got held by everyone as they said that, with a little tact and understanding, I might rate an honourable mention in the 'best teen' stakes.

So Joe's back to teeth picking, Kitty's back to daily visits and Mum's nostrils are continually dilated, as she fixes this phoney smile on her face and tells Kitty how good it is to see her.

'Hi, Kitty,' I call out.

'I bought you a present,' says Kitty, and she walks right into my bedroom, without asking, mind you. 'Actually it's for the garden really, but you might want to name her.'

Kitty has bought me a female garden gnome. I thought all gernomees were male but I must be wrong. This one is definitely female because she has boobs, red lips, long blonde hair curling under her pixie cap, and a kind of pixie tracksuit. She's holding a miniature watering can.

'Um, thanks, Kitty. I'll put her next to Ron. It'll cheer him up no end.'

'Yes, I thought he might like company.' While Kitty wanders through the house peeking into each and every corner, I take the female gernomee to the front garden. What will I call her? I know. I'll call her Georgia after 'Sweet Georgia Brown'.

I stand Georgia next to Ron, between the carnations. I let them face each other. I even go through preliminary introductions. 'Ron, meet Georgia, the love of your life. Georgia, this is Ron. Don't be put off by that silly grin on his face. He's quite okay, really.'

'Hey, Hatty, what on earth are you doing?'

It's Suzy and Giles. How embarrassing to be caught talking to garden gnomes. Giles stands near the front gate with a slight frown on his face. I know he thinks I'm a jerk, but I don't care. I've got my own column.

I invite them inside. Bad mistake. Kitty

Litter hovers around us in the kitchen like a helicopter looking for a place to land.

'I'll make you kids some chocolate malt milkshakes. My own recipe. Loads of malt and an egg thrown in.'

'An egg?' says Suzy, screwing up her face.

'Full of protein,' says Kitty.

I bring out the family photograph album, and the three of us pore over pictures while I try to select a really good shot for my column.

'That one's not bad,' says Giles, pointing to a head-and-shoulders shot Mum took of me to send to my dad in New Zealand. Mum liked it so much she had it reprinted.

'Don't know about that gap in your teeth,' says Suzy.

'It's part of who I am,' I protest. 'I think I look cute and Raymond will think so too.'

Kitty leans over the table. Wisps of grey hair tickle my face.

'That gap in your teeth makes you look more interesting, Hatty. It gives you character.'

I grin. Just occasionally Kitty shows very good taste.

'I'll take this one to Mr Bates,' I say, removing the photo from its hinges and sticking it in my pocket.

'You know Hatty,' says Giles. 'You're a bit weird at times and I've never seen anyone with your kind of crazy energy, but I've got to give it to you. You're going places with Hatty's Hotline.'

'She sure is,' says Kitty. 'She's going to be a household name, like Vegemite.'

The phone rings and Kitty goes to answer it. It's Joe. While they're talking Giles and Suzy crack up. 'Vegemite. Ha, ha.'

Suzy and Giles, still laughing hysterically, leave just as Mum arrives. She's been working back and is tired and grumpy. Seeing Kitty in the kitchen re-arranging the fridge magnets doesn't improve her mood.

'Oh, Kitty, it's you,' she says in a flat voice.

'Sure thing,' says Kitty cheerily.

'I'm a bit tired. I might just have a lie down,' says Mum.

'I'll start making the dinner,' says Kitty, helpfully, and she opens the fridge door.

'Good thinking, Kitty,' I say, as Mum trudges out of the room. 'Want me to peel the vegetables?'

'Sure thing,' says Kitty, flashing me a slightly yellow, toothy smile.

I take beans and carrots out of the vegetable crisper at the bottom of the fridge.

'How come you look at that photo of Aunt Harriet and Thomas so often?' I ask Kitty, as I see her glancing up at their picture.

Kitty puts a chopping board on the bench top near the sink.

'There's something about your great aunt and the way she looks at Thomas. That glow in her face. It reminds me of when I was young. The way I felt about my husband, Joe's dad. He was somebody.'

'You really miss him a lot, eh? Guess you and he really got on well together?'

'Well together? Oh, dear no, we argued most of the time. He was full of fire and brimstone. Me too. We had the most fantastic arguments, about almost anything. But then we made up. They were great times.'

'I guess he was really special, Kitty.'

'Hmm, did you say you want a roast or chops for dinner, Hatty?'

A tear glistens in the corner of Kitty's eye. A wave of guilt hits me. How could I have been so hard on her? She's so lonely.

It is at that moment that I get my brilliant idea. It is a great idea. It is creative. It will make everyone happy.

It is just bad luck that I forget I am holding the vegetable peeler and at that moment mistake my finger for a carrot.

Chapter Seven

'**I** can't stand it, Joe. I know I told you I'd try to be more understanding but I've had enough. It's not that I don't like your mother. She means well. But you and I need time together.'

'I thought we'd sorted this out. You're not being fair, Margaret. I don't tell Hatty to get lost every time I feel like being alone with you. We're a family now, and my mother's part of the family.'

'You can't compare gaining a stepdaughter to having a mother coming every day, *every single day*, Joe, to be with us. I may only have a part-time job but I'm still tired when I get home. And that's when I want to switch off. I don't want to see your mother's grinning face at the front door. Honestly, I don't understand it. Before we got married she must have had a life.'

'She did, but it was at the retirement village. She moved to be closer to us because she was so thrilled that I'd finally settled down. She's got no friends round here yet. Just us. And she's so fond of you. And of Hatty. In time she'll settle down, and then we'll see less of her. But for the time being, she's my mum, and I reckon she can come here whenever she likes.'

'You don't understand, Joe. She's taking over. She's even arranged all the cans in the pantry in lines according to their size. That might not sound like a problem but I had my own system and I can't find a thing.'

'She's a very neat person. She just wants to help. You've just got to be more patient.'

'Is that your final word on the subject, Joe?'

'It sure is, and I must say I'm very disappointed in you, Margaret.'

'And I'm very disappointed in you, Joe.'

'Raymond, I'd love to come and see you play at Swaggers, but if I don't get my homework done Miss Jerome is going to kill me.'

'It's not your homework, it's Hatty's Hotline, isn't it? Even if you really have to do your homework it's only because you've been working so hard on your column that you're behind in your school-work. Look, Hatty, I reckon it's great that you've got this job with the paper, but when do I get to see you? And what about going to the movies on Saturday?

I thought we had a definite arrangement with Giles and Suzy.'

'We do. We did. But there are all these letters that I have to answer personally. And, you know, Raymond, I get fan mail as well.'

'Well can't you send them a printed thank-you card.'

'That's just *so* impolite. I can't believe you just said that Raymond. And I always thought you were a caring person.'

'Well, maybe I'm just an ordinary person, Hatty, who wants to see more of his girlfriend.'

'Oh yeah?'

'Yeah.'

Mum and I sit on garden chairs in our front garden. Ron and Georgia are eyeing each other between the carnations. The late afternoon sun makes me squint. Mum's eyes are hidden by dark glasses, but I suspect she's been crying. My own eyes feel fine thank you, but I am angry.

'Raymond is just so, so insensitive.'

'Joe doesn't seem to realise we've only been married five minutes and the romance is already going out of our marriage.'

'I always thought Raymond was so special, and here he is carrying on and on about my column. I reckon he's jealous.'

'Joe puts his mother before me every time.

Last week, she even re-arranged my fridge magnets. It just won't do.'

'He expects me to come to every one of his gigs, and yet he resents the time I spend writing for Hatty's Hotline.'

'I'm going to have a talk with Kitty and put it on the line with Joe. She can come over three times a week and she's to stop moving things around. If that's not good enough for the two of them, well, well . . . I just might have to do something drastic.'

'I'm going to tell Raymond that he's got to shape up or ship out. This column is the greatest opportunity I've ever had. He's got to be more understanding or I'll have to do something drastic.'

'Thanks for listening to me, Hatty. You've been very supportive.'

'And thanks for listening to me, Mum. Now I've talked this over with you, I see things clearly.'

'So, you're saying that I'm jealous of you? Are you nuts, Hatty? I just want to see more of you.'

'Well, I'm sick and tired of you putting pressure on me. It's not as if I don't support you. It's not like I don't come to your gigs. I've only missed the last two.'

'It's not just the gigs. It's the way I'm low

down on your list of priorities, Hatty. Can't you compromise? I have to do my homework at really weird times so I can be with you the next day. Have you thought of getting someone to help you answer your letters?'

'Oh yeah, Raymond. I can just see Mr Bates employing a secretary for me. Anyway, my letters are very private. No one else can add that special personal touch. I owe it to the kids out there.'

'Well, maybe you owe me a bit of your time as well, Hatty.'

'You know what, Raymond? If that's the way you feel, maybe we should have a break from each other.'

'Oh yeah?'

'Yeah.'

The phone clicks. I'm boiling with anger. Mum, gritting her teeth, has gone to the movies with Joe and Kitty, and I'm home alone. I'd love to rant and rave to Mum now about how insensitive Raymond is, but I can't.

I storm off into the kitchen. There's this tight feeling in my stomach. But Raymond had it coming. He's just been off his tree since I got this column.

I stare up at Aunt Harriet. 'I always thought it was a pity you two didn't hit the jackpot and end up together, but maybe it was all for the best. So stop looking at Thomas in that sloppy way, Aunt Harriet.'

I open a packet of biscuits. Raymond was so special. How could he have changed so much? Why am I sitting in front of a packet of chocolate biscuits and not wanting to eat any? Those trees in the park. The day we kissed beside each tree. How long will our 'break' last? I'm missing him already. Maybe I should write a letter to Hatty's Hotline and see what advice I can give myself.

'You've broken up with Raymond? You've broken up with Raymond?' Suzy's voice is squeaky. 'You've actually broken up with Raymond?'

'You don't have to keep repeating it,' I say, twisting the telephone cord nervously. 'We're just having a – a break from each other. That's not the same as actually "breaking up".'

'You're having a "break" from each other?'

'Suzy, can you stop repeating everything I say? It's just a break.'

'A break? It's just a break?'

'Suzy, quit repeating everything I say or I'll hang up.'

'You'll hang up? Okay, don't hang up. You've just shocked me so much. I thought Raymond and you were a top item. Well, up until about six weeks ago.'

'What happened six weeks ago?'

'What happened six weeks ago? Sorry, don't put the phone down. Honestly, Hatty, for someone who's writing an advice column you're amazingly stupid. You took on Hatty's Hotline and dumped your friends. That's what happened.'

'I did not.'

'You did so. You hardly ever call me. You never come round. You're not interested in anything I'm doing. If I didn't come by to see you, we'd only meet at school. And Raymond? Well, Giles and I have been to his last two gigs. You should see his face when he plays. He stares at where you used to sit and he looks like one of those dogs with the droopy eyes – a cocker spaniel, I think.'

'But, but I'm busy.'

'He is too, but he always made time for you. You're carried away with your column, Hatty. We're all happy for you. But you're taking on more than you can handle. If you're going to continue writing the Hotline you need someone to help you.'

'I've got a duty to my fans.'

'Your fans? What about your friends? What about Raymond?'

'You're exaggerating, Suzy. Every relationship has its ups and downs. I bet you have problems with Giles too.'

'Sure. He's crazy about football, and all I know about it is that it has something to do with feet and a ball. I go and watch him play footy even though I'd rather be at the beach. And he doesn't like jazz at all, but he still comes along to Raymond's gigs, even though he fidgets all the time. And . . .'

'Okay, I get your point.' I'm starting to feel pit-of-the-stomach sick. Usually when I'm moody I get terrible hunger pangs. Now, I don't feel hungry at all. No appetite. I may never eat again. I could be getting some awful illness. Then again, maybe I just feel guilty.

I say goodbye to Suzy and sit on the sofa, twiddling with a loose thread on the cushion cover. Suzy's my best friend, but deep down I always thought she was an airhead and I was the deep and meaningful one. When the four of us went out, Suzy always looked for mirrors or shop windows and then she'd stop and check herself out. She's the type that guys drool over, so I couldn't understand why she'd bother to do this. I never check myself out because all I'd see would be this slightly plump, average-looking, pleasant-faced girl with a healthy gap between her front teeth, staring back at me.

I'm not the stuff that movie stars are made of, but that's okay. At least I'm average and

Raymond likes me just the way I am. Or the way I was.

Yet it's Suzy who's got insight, and me, with my big, full-page column, and my growing mound of letters, who may turn out to be the airhead.

I hear voices outside the front door. That's strange. The movie won't be over for ages. The key turns and the door creaks open.

'How could you say that to my mother? How could you?'

'Joe, you've got to make a choice. It's your mother or me. I can't take it any more. I've tried, honestly, but she's with us all the time.'

'Telling her to get herself a life, and criticising her for arranging the books on the shelf in alphabetical order.'

'I was very tactful. I just couldn't find my Harold Robbins book. She'd filed it under 'H' not 'R'. It was just a question.'

'Did you see her lower jaw tremble? She was in shock.'

'Joe, it's a family trait. Your lower jaw shakes when you're that way.'

I sneak out the back door into the garden. I sit on the cool grass, study the lacework pattern of stars in the sky and try not to listen to the two of them carrying on. But you'd have to wear ear plugs over your ear plugs to block out the sound.

'If you'd just give her time to make new friends, Margaret.'

'How's she going to make friends if she hangs around us all the time?'

'When my dad died I was just a kid. I hardly remember him. She worked long hours to help me make something of myself. You don't know how hard it was for her.'

'I've been a single parent as well. I do know.'

'That was different. You were divorced. My dad died.'

'It wasn't so different, Joe. I didn't want a divorce. I loved my husband long after the divorce was through. I even kept an urn in the lounge room filled with earth from my old family garden. Remember?'

'Of course I remember. I was with you when you finally threw the earth out – or have you forgotten? What are you implying? Are you trying to tell me that you're still in love with your ex-husband?'

'Right now he's looking pretty good.'

'Oh, really?'

'Really.'

I hear Joe's heavy tread as he marches away from Mum. I should go inside but I don't want to right now. All these problems. I stare at the night sky, at the stars wheeling their way benignly around the universe. I wonder about life on other planets. Perhaps, at this very moment, Mr XXZ on the planet Zifflehump at the far side of the galaxy, is telling Mrs XXZ off for not getting on with her mother-in-law.

I listen to the neighbour's cat squealing. A dog barking somewhere. A police siren wailing in the distance. What's Raymond doing now? Is he feeling miserable, too?

'Hatty? Hat – tee?' Mum's calling me.

'Here, Mum. In the back garden.'

The back door opens and Mum walks out to me. 'What are you doing sitting on the grass? You'll get a chill.' She shrugs and sits down beside me.

A cool breeze rocks the dark shape of the wattle tree at the end of the garden. Silvery light dapples the grass. Crickets hum as Mum and I huddle together in shared misery.

'Why is life so complicated, Mum?'

'I don't know, Hatty. I suppose you heard Joe and I having a go at each other.'

'Yes, and I want you to know that I think you're completely right, even though Kitty's not such a bad old girl.'

'Joe's moving out.'

'Joe's moving out?' I turn and face Mum. I can't see her clearly in the darkness, just the outline of her profile. Her voice is calm.

'Just for a week or so.'

'For a week or so?'

'Hatty, stop repeating what I say. Joe says he wants to think things out.'

'What does he have to think out? What does Kitty Litter have to say about all this?'

'I don't know Hatty, and don't call her that. I think she really did try to understand when I spoke to her over dinner, but I hurt her feelings and Joe's having trouble coming to terms with that.'

'Well, I'll have more time, so I'll look after you if you need someone to talk to. By the way, I'm not seeing Raymond right now.'

'You're not seeing Raymond right now? What happened?'

'Nothing. It's like with you and Joe. It's not forever. It's just a break.'

'A break?'

'Mum, can you stop repeating everything I say? Look, I don't want to talk about it, right now. I'm going to my room. My bum's freezing.'

I jump up and run inside. Mum and I have really big problems. I should write myself a letter immediately.

It's hard to concentrate on Hatty's Hotline. Hard to look at the jumbled pile of mail on the end of my bed and make sense of the other kids' problems. I'm missing Raymond. Maybe this break from him has been long enough. But he hasn't phoned me, so maybe he doesn't miss me. What can I do? What advice would I get from Hatty's Hotline?

I sift vaguely through my letters, trying to muster interest. It's then I remember that letter from Victor. I had a great idea, but what with all the breaking up going on in the house, I'd forgotten.

Let's see. Victor has conveniently given me his full name and address. Victor Katt. And he lives locally. I'm going to push Raymond from my mind and give Victor a call.

Chapter Eight

It's Saturday, and I'm sitting on a wrought-iron bench at the park. It's the same park where Raymond and I set our kissing record. All the baby trees are nodding gently in the late afternoon breeze, and seem to be growing nicely. My stomach goes into spasms just watching them. Raymond still hasn't phoned me. Should I call him? What if he tells me to get lost?

I've got to put thoughts of Raymond behind me now or I'll never get this right.

A small boy walking a dog comes strolling up to where I'm sitting. He's about twelve or so, wearing a pair of faded jeans and a striped t-shirt, and on his head is a navy-blue baseball cap turned on one side. He's skinny with a bony face and a sprinkling of freckles.

'Hatty?' he says. 'I recognised you from your photo in the paper. Wow! I still can't believe this.'

The dog, a wagging labrador, jumps up on me and gives me a wet lick on my cheek.

'This is Sandy,' says Victor. 'He can't believe it, either. Hey, Sandy, we're meeting a real celebrity.' I wince because the halo that had been circling my head has a big dent in it. I pat Sandy. Victor sits next to me and tosses a ball for Sandy to run after.

'Well, what are we going to do?' asks Victor.

What's led up to this meeting? On Thursday afternoon I spoke to Victor after finding his phone number in the local directory. A gruff elderly voice on the other end told me to hang on, and then Victor came to the phone.

He was so excited when I said who I was it was embarrassing.

'You give all that awesome advice in your column. Honest. I'm so impressed.'

When he'd recovered from being impressed I told him about my plan. How we'd solve two problems with the one hit.

He listened carefully, just stopping every now and then to say, 'This is very cool. This is just so great.'

So we arranged to meet, and I asked him not to discuss anything with his parents or his grandfather because they'd think we were interfering busybodies, which of course we weren't, were we?

'Joe's mother, I guess that makes her my step-grandmother, is about seventy-five or so,' I tell Victor. 'She's little, okay-looking for an oldie, and doesn't have any friends apart from us.

'She's not a bad sort, but she comes around all the time. And she interferes. She came into my bedroom once and re-arranged all the clothing in my wardrobe. I had this untidy order that was perfect. Now all my tops are in one neat line, and I can't find a thing.'

'Wow! If my grandad re-arranged my wardrobe my mum would give him a medal,' says Victor. 'He just sits around tapping time to his daggy music. He listens to this classical stuff. And it's so loud. When Mum and Dad come home from work he turns it down but he's got no consideration for me. I could end up with serious ear damage.'

'And Kitty's bought yellow cushions for our sofa because she's *very* into the colour yellow. That's really inconsiderate. We were quite happy with our old cushions.'

'She bought you yellow cushions? If my grandad bought us cushions, my mother would bring out a thermometer because he doesn't even want to go as far as the corner shop.'

'So you see, I reckon Kitty isn't a bad old stick at all. She just needs someone in her life, someone to think about apart from us, and she'll be fine.'

'You're right,' says Victor. 'And I reckon that if my grandad met someone who turned him on, he'd turn his music off and be a happier person, and maybe we could go fishing and play Monopoly again.'

'Right now, my stepfather, Joe, has moved back in with his mum. He's annoyed because we don't want Kitty to visit all the time.'

'She definitely needs a boyfriend,' says Victor. Sandy places a spit-covered ball in Victor's palm. 'Here, go chase, Sandy.' Victor throws the ball and Sandy dashes off.

'So, this is what we're going to do, Victor.'

I arrive home feeling hopeful. This will work. I won't goof this up like I did when I tried to arrange a mail-order boyfriend for Mum. I stare at Ron, the garden gnome. He's definitely getting keen on Georgia. Next thing you know, they'll be dating. But it's too soon, and she may need time out. I pick her up from the earth and take her to the back garden under the wattle tree. She needs a break from Ron. He's coming on too strong.

On Friday, after four painful days apart, during which time he and Mum make frantic, and sometimes sloppy, phone calls to each other, Joe leaves Kitty's flat and moves back home.

Joe seems happy to see me. He walks cautiously down the hall carrying a small suitcase, a bunch of flowers and a box of Maltesers.

Mum has sprayed herself with a lethal dose of perfume, and I am choking from the fumes. She's also bought a big apple pie from the cake shop.

I look carefully behind Joe as he moves down the hall. Where's Kitty? She's been his little shadow for so long, it seems strange to see Joe by himself.

'How's things, Hatty,' Joes says to me. 'Here, something to help you concentrate while you write your column.'

'Thanks, Joe,' I say, as he hands me a huge box of Maltesers. I give him an awkward hug. 'I sort of missed you.'

'My mother had a good talk with me, Hatty.' Joe hugs me back, then says, in a low voice, 'She agreed with your mum that she'd been overdoing things. I could whack myself for reacting the way I did.'

'Joe?' calls Mum.

Mum is definitely a health hazard. The fumes from her perfume are toxic and my eyes are watering. She's had her hair curled and it looks like a lot of electrocuted wires around her face. Her lips and cheeks are bright pink, and I can see by the look she gives Joe that I am in for a lot of mush, which I can't cope with right now.

So I leave them alone while they go in for the big kiss, and sit at the end of my bed, watching a bird doing a plop on my window ledge.

Raymond? Why hasn't he called? Should I make the first move or wait for him to contact me? I can't stand the uncertainty. I ignore the mush taking place in the kitchen, take the plunge and phone Raymond.

'Raymond's gone out,' says his mum. Out? Where's he gone? Is he seeing someone else? I pull nervously at the telephone cord. 'Well, Hatty, actually he's in but he's got a large sign on his door that says, 'I'm not home'. I don't know if you'd call that "in" or "out".'

'Tell him it's me, Mrs Dobie,' I plead.

'What's with you two?' she asks.

'We're, um, having a break from each other.'

'A break?'

'Just for a while.'

'A while?'

I wriggle and squirm. What's wrong with everyone? Can't two teenagers decide to cool it without the world going nuts?

Mrs Dobie goes to see whether Raymond is 'in' or 'out'. I wait for ages. Finally, I hear that voice I know and love.

'Um, Hatty.' His voice is thin and flat. 'How've you been?'

'Fine. You?'

'Fine.'

Hey, what's happening here? We've never been stuck for conversation. The words are stuttering out of us.

'How's the music?'

'Fine. And your column?'

'Fine.' I can't stand it. I blink away something moist that is fogging my eyes. 'Thought I'd just, um, give you a call.'

'Thanks.'

'Whoops, got to go. The timer's buzzing on the stove. If I don't move the spuds the smoke alarm will go off, and then the fire brigade will turn up. Um, goodbye Raymond.'

I put the phone down. Imagine. I had to tell a whopper because the conversation was as dry as the Sahara. I watch as Joe and Mum walk down the hall in a mushy haze. This is getting seriously nauseating.

Maybe the trees in the park will be full-grown before Raymond and I make up properly. Maybe I'll be writing Hatty's Geriatric Column by then. Maybe I should go and have a talk with Aunt Harriet. Then again, Kitty's probably feeling low, so maybe I should pay her a visit.

'It's nice of you to come over, Hatty. A real treat,' says Kitty. 'Come and sit down and we'll have a cosy chat.'

There are wind chimes next to Kitty's back door and they tinkle pleasantly. Yellow curtains hang in the window and numerous tiny garden gnomes sit on the kitchen window sill. I stare at the photo of Kitty's parents.

'Kitty, how come there isn't a picture of your late husband anywhere around?'

'Lemonade or Coca Cola, Hatty?'

'Lemonade. Did you hear what I said?'

'I've got my photographs, and my memories too, but I only take out the photos from time to time, because of the pain, you see. I really miss Joe's dad. Never quite got over him. Such a fiery man. Full of passion. Oh well, that's life. One lamington or two?'

'Would you come for a walk with me on Sunday afternoon, Kitty? We could go to the park.'

'Isn't that when Raymond plays the piano?'

I feel my cheeks go hot. 'Actually, we're having a break from each other.'

'A break?'

'Just a little break. Just for a week or maybe two.'

'A week or maybe two?'

'Kitty, please don't repeat everything I say. Why does everyone get so worked up when I say Raymond and I are having a teeny holiday from each other?'

'Because you're so good together, that's why, Hatty,' says Kitty. 'Here, try my lamingtons. My own recipe. Always go heavy on the coconut, that's what I say. You take care of Raymond, Hatty. He's a special person. You are, too. It'd be a terrible waste if you split up. You've only got to ask your aunt.'

'She's just a picture on a wall, Kitty.'

'Dear me, you are in a bad way, Hatty,' says Kitty, and she smiles. 'Yes, I'd be happy to come for a walk with you on Sunday. And thanks for dropping by. Your mum's invited me over for dinner next week, but I won't be coming round like I did before. And I won't be re-lining the kitchen cupboards or arranging the coat hangers so they face due north. Frankly though, I think I did a very good job in making your house tidy.'

I stare at her and bite my lip, then shrug and bite into the lamington. Kitty is a very good cook. It's no wonder she had a cooking column when she was young.

My mind ticks over. Some time between now and Sunday I have to suss out Victor's grandfather. Give him a good looking over. After all, I'm not going to introduce Kitty to just anyone. He's got to be special.

Chapter Nine

Victor's street is about ten minutes by bus from my place. The house is very cute. It's painted green, has lots of leafy shrubs, and sweet-smelling jasmine snakes around the front porch. Victor has invited me around to meet his grandfather, Arthur. His parents are both working, so it gives me a chance to thoroughly scrutinise old Arthur and make sure he is *the* one.

I walk up the winding path to the front door. A barking Sandy trots up to me from the side of the house with a dripping ball in his mouth.

'G'day, Sandy,' I say, as I lean over and pat his head. I then stand tall, take a deep breath and ring the front door buzzer.

Victor opens the door. He winks at me. 'I've chipped a tooth since I last saw you. I walked into a shelf at the supermarket. We might sue the store. Come in.'

We troop down a small sunny hallway. A

growling voice says, 'Who's there, Victor? Has your mum come home early?'

'No, it's my friend, Hatty,' Victor calls back. He leads me into a dining room. An elderly man sits tapping his fingers on a large shiny table. The classical music he's listening to is very loud. Victor is right. His ear-drums could be in serious danger.

'This is Hatty, Grandad.'

Victor's grandfather nods at me. 'How d'you do?'

Arthur has a thick thatch of white hair, bright pink skin and a deep furrow between his eyes. White curly hair spouts from his large ears. Small glasses sit nervously at the end of his nose. He peers over them at me.

'Didn't know Victor liked older women,' he booms, over the music.

'She's helping me with my homework, Grandad,' says Victor.

'Well, don't just stand there, Victor. Get the young lady a glass of lemonade. Unless you'd prefer whiskey.' His voice is deadly serious.

'Um, lemonade will do just fine,' I say.

Victor brings me a drink. I drink quickly. Arthur continues to eye me, then he turns away and taps the table. He's totally hooked on the music.

'Don't suppose you like the classics?' he asks.

'I'm more into jazz. Don't suppose you like jazz?'

'What's that you said?' He cups a hand to one ear.

'Jazz,' I yell above the music. 'Don't suppose you like jazz?'

'Hate it. It's raucous and far too loud. I can't bear trumpets and drums. I like Beethoven and Chopin.'

'You mean Beetroot and Chopsticks?' says Victor.

'Don't try to be funny, Victor. If you listened to my music instead of that junk *you* listen to, you'd learn a thing or two.'

'Yeah, yeah, yeah,' says Victor.

'And get Hatty a coaster. Where are your manners?'

Victor gives me a 'you see what I mean' look and comes back with a small coaster. Arthur continues to beat time to the music. Violins cry. Cellos wail. Victor groans.

'Why can't I put on some of my type of music, Grandad? If you listened to Smashing Pumpkins for a change, it might do you good.'

'Any group with a name like "Smashing Pumpkins" has a problem. Anyway, your kind of music pollutes your ears,' shouts Arthur, as the orchestra blasts away.

'Does not,' Victor shouts back.

'Hmm. Didn't you say that Hatty was here to help you with your homework?'

I gulp down my drink, and get up from my chair. Arthur nods briefly at me, then goes back to tapping his fingers on the table.

Victor and I go to his room. He has football posters on the wall, and piles of books and comics strewn over the floor. 'It's a mess,' he says. 'Maybe I should get your Kitty to organise it. Well, what did you think of Grandad? He's pretty painful, isn't he?'

'He's okay,' I say. 'He's a bit short-tempered, but I think that's because he's lonely. Like Kitty. I reckon it's a goer.'

Victor grins. 'Now I've just got to talk him into going for a walk to the park. Maybe I could say there's going to be a concert there, and that all his favourite music will be on.'

'Victor, you're a very talented liar.'

Sunday afternoon.

'I'm really bucked that you and Kitty are going for a walk together,' says Joe, his face twitching with emotion. 'By the way, have you noticed something, Hatty?'

'Um, no, Joe. What?'

'My knuckles. I'm trying to stop cracking them. But if you miss the noise, ha, ha, I can always start again.'

'No, Joe,' I say quickly. 'I was wondering why

the place was so quiet. But I was enjoying the silence. Honest.'

'The tooth-picking is a long-standing habit. I know it's aggravating. Your mum doesn't really like it either, but I can't break that one in a hurry, Hatty, though I'll certainly work on it. I guess we've all got our funny ways. I've caught you talking to that picture of your Aunt Harriet.'

'I don't do it often . . .' I protest.

'You mean, I don't catch you often,' says Joe, and he claps me on the back and roars with laughter. 'Anyway, give my love to my dear old mum when you see her, and tell her we'll expect her for dinner tomorrow night.'

Is it really Sunday afternoon? My heart is positioned somewhere near my navel. At this very moment, Raymond is running his fingers over the piano keys at his gig. He hasn't phoned me since *that* phone call and I haven't phoned him. The silence is pure torture.

As I walk up the path, I mutter a quick goodbye to Ron, the garden gernomee, as he stares silently around him. He's looking a bit miserable. Maybe I should bring Georgia back to keep him company.

'I've brought a basket of lamingtons along for us to nibble on,' Kitty Litter tells me.

I've collected Kitty and we're walking along her street. She's wearing a red short-sleeved jumper and matching tracksuit bottoms. She has a red scarf tied around her neck, and a basket draped over her arm. If she wore the scarf on her head she'd look like Little Red Riding Hood.

'It's a lovely park,' I tell her. 'They've planted a lot of new trees, and there's a stream there where I used to catch tadpoles when I was little. Oh, and we might run into Victor. He's this kid I know. He might be taking a walk there as well.'

'That's nice, Hatty,' says Kitty. 'I've got plenty of lamingtons for us all.'

We cross the road, walk down a few side streets and arrive at the park. My stomach knots as I look around. All the tiny trees, waving their teeny branches, remind me of that wonderful day when Raymond and I kissed meaningfully beside each and every one of them. Afterwards, my lips were happily raw. Now, they're healed and unloved. Raymond, where are you?

We make our way across the velvet grass. It's been raining almost every night and the grass is a lush shade of emerald. We pass garden beds, with brightly coloured flowers bobbing their heads. It's all very pretty.

'Hey, Hatty.' It's Victor. He's running across

the park with Sandy beside him. Arthur is strolling behind them.

'Is that your friend Victor?' asks Kitty. 'And who's that man with him?'

Victor comes charging across to us. Unfortunately, Sandy jumps up on Kitty excitedly and the basket goes tumbling over. A dozen perfectly good lamingtons lie scattered like wounded soldiers, and before you can say 'drat that dog', Sandy's mouth is in the grass and he's scoffing them up.

'Oh dear,' says Kitty, shaking her head, as I grab the basket from Sandy's jaws. 'But there are still a lot left.'

Arthur has now made his way to us. 'That stupid mutt. I told Victor to leave him at home. Hello, Hatty.' He nods at Kitty.

'Kitty, um, this is Victor – and his grandfather, Arthur. Arthur meet Kitty.'

The two oldies shake hands awkwardly. Kitty squints at Arthur, who is staring around him. 'Hatty,' he says to me. 'I believe there's going to be an open-air classical music concert here.'

'I didn't know about that,' says Kitty.

'Um, I think you've got your parks mixed up,' I say seriously to Victor. 'That, um, concert was at Hyde Park, wasn't it?' While Arthur stands looking confused, I point to a vacant park bench. 'How about we sit down and finish what's left of the lamingtons before Sandy makes another dive for them.'

Which is what we do, but the silence between Arthur and Kitty is uncomfortable. Kitty, who is an avid talker, has suddenly gone quiet. Arthur is still looking around as if he's expecting a one-hundred-piece symphony orchestra to materialise from behind the trees.

'I wouldn't have come if I'd known,' he says to Victor. 'There was a superb concert on Channel 2.'

'I prefer jazz myself,' says Kitty unhelpfully.

'I like Smashing Pumpkins,' adds Victor, even more unhelpfully.

'Dear me, that's an odd hobby,' says Kitty.

'I'm sort of "middle of the road",' I say.

So there we sit, while kids swing on swings, and parents wheel babies in strollers. Victor throws a ball for Sandy to run after. Arthur's face is creased into a big frown. I stare at my shoelaces and wonder whether I should tie them together for something to do.

Finally, Kitty says, 'This park needs a bit more colour. I think rows of daffodils in that garden bed over there would bring a real splash to this park.'

'I prefer roses,' says Arthur.

'Want a lamington?' asks Kitty, fishing in her basket.

'Not usually, but I'll try one.'

Arthur eats one of Kitty's delicious lamingtons. Victor and I also take one and exchange quick, secret smiles. Finally, there's a small crack in Arthur's shell. Things are looking up.

Unfortunately, Arthur then proceeds to choke on one of Kitty's lamingtons. He starts to cough and wheeze and his face turns bright red.

'Good grief,' says Kitty. 'Quick, Hatty, bang him on the back.'

I jump up and give him a quick thump on his back. It doesn't seem to help. He continues to cough loudly and his eyes fill up with tears.

I give him another thump. This time, his glasses drop off his nose.

'It's the coconut,' says Victor. He also gives his grandfather a hard thump. 'It's gone down the wrong way.'

'I'm . . . choking,' Arthur gasps.

'Don't worry, Arthur,' says Kitty. 'You'll live.' She leaps up and punches him hard between his ribs. Then, she gives him a huge wallop on the back with her bag. He splutters and coughs, and suddenly a few shreds of coconut fly out of his distorted mouth. He stops coughing. His ragged jerky breath slowly evens out. Finally, while we all stare anxiously, he puts his hand in his pocket, takes out a handkerchief and wipes his eyes. He takes a deep breath.

'I think you've broken my ribs,' he says to Kitty. 'Those blasted lamingtons. Too much coconut in them.'

'It improves the flavour,' says Kitty, indignantly. 'That's a nasty thing to say about my lamingtons. It's not my fault you've got a skinny windpipe.'

'I don't like lamingtons, and I thought I was coming to a concert,' says Arthur. 'And I don't like daffodils, and there's nothing wrong with the size of my windpipe. And I want my glasses.'

Kitty stands back. There is a crunching sound.

'You foolish woman. You've broken my specs.'

Kitty removes her shoe from what is left of Arthur's glasses.

'Well, you could say I also saved your life. If we'd left you to choke you wouldn't have had much use for your glasses,' she says. 'You're a very rude man.'

'I want to go home, Victor,' says Arthur. 'Right now. You'll have to show me the way out of this park. Thanks to this silly woman, I can't see a blasted thing.'

Victor and I exchange very worried looks. This is not working out at all. Kitty stands up, holds her head very high and says to me, 'It's time we left too. Coming, Hatty?'

'Um . . .' I say.

Arthur stretches himself to his full height, which is about a head and a half taller than Kitty.

'Coming, Victor?'

'Um . . .' says Victor.

We set off in different directions. Victor, giving me one last frantic stare, leads his grandfather past the garden beds. Kitty and I set off past the baby trees.

Kitty suddenly turns and yells to Arthur, 'And I suppose you don't like garden gnomes?'

'Hate them,' he yells back.

Kitty and I trudge out of the park. In the far distance, I can see Victor and his grandad disappearing from view.

'That was awful,' I say to Kitty. 'I can't believe how rude he was.'

'Blue eyes,' says Kitty. 'Did you notice how blue his eyes are? Such a temper. Joe's dad was like that when I first met him. Before I tamed him.'

'What are you saying, Kitty?'

'All that huffing and puffing about my lamingtons. He did that to catch my attention. I could tell.'

'He did?'

'I think I'll ask Arthur over for dinner. Yes indeed, that's what I'll do.'

'Huh?'

Chapter Ten

'So you see, Margaret, my policy in life has always been "nothing ventured nothing gained".' (Kitty Litter, winding spaghetti around her fork, over dinner.)

'But Kitty, from what Hatty says, this man, Arthur, was rude and insulting.' (Mum, twiddling with a stray curl and wearing a slight frown.)

'He's interested in me. I can tell. And you and Joe have repeatedly told me how I need another interest in my life.'

'Yes, but gosh Mum, this fellow sounds like he needs a good kick up the . . .' (Joe, agitated, and ready to make a citizen's arrest on Arthur.)

'Joe, don't talk that way.' (Mum, refined and genteel, with a coil of spaghetti stuck to her chin.)

I sigh. Got to get back to the computer. Got to get round to reading all those letters. Hatty's Hotline continues to be a great success and Mr Bates is very pleased with me.

'Hatty,' he told me, when I last went to the office. 'The letters roll in. We're getting more advertisers than ever for our little suburban paper. You're becoming a household name.' Then he handed me two huge bags of mail and a long glass of water because I'd turned pale.

No word from Raymond. What if he's found someone else? Anything's possible. It happened to Aunt Harriet. Imagine if another girl, one with skinnier hips than me, is sipping lemonade and going starry-eyed as Raymond plays 'Sweet Georgia Brown'.

'Don't worry. Raymond likes you just the way you are,' says Suzy. 'You don't know how lucky you are. Giles is okay, but he's very into the way I look. Fortunately, I'm very into the way I look too, so there's no conflict there. You're stubborn and nuts, Hatty. So's Raymond, but you're more stubborn and definitely nuttier. He's the proud, silent type. He wants you back, but you've got to make time for him. He always made time for you. You're the one who wouldn't budge. He won't come crawling.'

'No one's telling him to come crawling. A simple phone call and an "I love you, Hatty" wouldn't be crawling.'

'You asked for this break. He didn't. Why don't you call him again and arrange to meet?'

'I don't know. Everything's going wrong – except for Mum and Joe. They're so happy I reckon they might have an annual marriage ceremony just for the fun of it. I get so tired. Last night, after I'd finished my homework, I was up until three in the morning sorting out letters for the column. If I see Raymond and we patch things up, maybe in a week's time I'll be busy with the Hotline and have no time for him and we'll start fighting again.'

'You're going to crack up if you don't take a break, Hatty. We're going ice-skating on Saturday afternoon. Want to come?'

'Are you joking? I've got two weeks of letters from desperate kids that I haven't even read.'

'Hatty, I think you're a desperate kid, too,' says Suzy.

'So, what do you reckon I should do, Aunt Harriet? And why are you looking at Thomas like that? Can't you give me a bit of your time?'

I'm in the kitchen, moodily talking to my aunt. Mum and Joe haven't come home from work yet. Kitty is at her place. So far, Arthur has totally rejected any suggestion that he go there for dinner, but she is not put off and keeps asking.

I can't believe I'm saying this, but I miss having her around so often. I miss finding the spoons all stacked one inside the other. Even

Mum said the other day that it wasn't such a bad idea of Kitty's to put all the books in alphabetical order. Then she shook her head and said, 'Did I just say what I thought I said, Hatty?'

I wander out into the garden. Georgia, the female gernomee, is standing under the wattle tree. A sprinkling of wattle covers her peaked cap.

'You look lonely,' I tell her. 'I think it's time we moved you back to Ron.'

So I pick Georgia up, walk around the side of the house, and place her next to Ron, between the carnations. I turn them so they face each other. Ron's fixed smile suddenly broadens when he sees Georgia. I blink. I really am stressed out. Raymond, where are you?

The phone rings. Raymond? Just maybe . . . I dash inside and pick it up. 'Is that you, Hatty? This is Bill Bates.'

'Oh yes. Hi, Mr Bates,' I say flatly.

'Hatty, I've been thinking about starting a cookery column. You remember those Anzac biscuits you brought over the other week?'

'Yes.' I'd taken over a huge bag for the staff at the office, for strictly selfish reasons. Kitty had baked heaps, and I was compulsively eating them. It was a question of sharing the calories or becoming a mountain.

'Do you think Kitty would be interested in writing a cookery column, on a trial basis? Mind you I think it could do quite well. She was well-known years ago. My mother remembers her column. In fact, it's possible I was brought up on recipes from Kitty's Korner. The salary wouldn't be huge to begin with, but I can discuss that with her. What do you think?'

'Wow, Mr Bates,' I say, and, from a totally lethargic state, I suddenly become so excited I manage to wind the telephone cord around my neck, strangling myself.

'What's that gurgling noise, Hatty?'

I manage to untangle the telephone cord before my air supply is totally cut off. 'I'll speak to her. I reckon she'll be out-of-her-brain keen.'

Then I hesitate. I'm not thinking clearly. This is not a good time to say anything rash. Raymond? Aunt Harriet? Am I saying the right thing? The words quickly fall from my mouth.

'Mr Bates, there's something I've got to discuss with you. It's my Hotline. I'm getting all this homework, and what with my column, I just don't have any time to see, um, special people in my life.'

'Hatty, you're not saying that you're . . .'

'No, I want to keep doing it, but do you think I could write it, say, every fortnight, and have a friend of mine, who is really very smart, giving advice the week I'm off? I've got to ask her first, but I wanted your opinion.'

There's a pause at the other end. I listen to the background jumble of computers buzzing and telephones ringing. My heart races. I may lose my Hotline.

'Hatty,' Mr Bates says, finally. 'I want you to do the Hotline, but I don't want you to burn yourself out. Hmm.'

I hold my breath. 'If there's no choice we can give it a go. I'll need to speak to your friend and to see how well she writes. What's her name?'

'Suzy. It could be called Suzy's Hotline on the weeks when I don't do it.'

'And she's smart, you say?'

'You better believe it.'

'Okay, Hatty. You speak to Kitty and your friend and tell them to contact me.'

I put the phone down and sink into the billowing warmth of the sofa. I hug a cushion. There's this deep sense of relief. Hatty and Suzy's Hotline. Can I share the Hotline? Can my ego take some minor bruising?

I phone Suzy and ask her if she's interested in writing the column on alternate weeks, though I don't have any real doubts. Firstly, she's my best friend and she's keen to save my life. Secondly, we can work together on this, and that'd be serious fun. And thirdly, there's a good chance they'll put her photo in the paper on the weeks when her column is printed.

'Hatty,' she screams down the phone, when I tell her my plan. 'This is so great, I'm going to pass out from shock. Weasel, stop jumping on my toes or I'll kill you. No, on second thought, now that I'm going to run a help column I won't kill you. I'll just send you away for intensive psychotherapy.'

I put the phone down, and bite my nails. Should I phone Raymond or should I wait? Maybe I should write a letter to Suzy and ask her? I am so confused.

The phone rings. This is proving to be a hectic day in the life of our phone. It's Victor.

'Thought I'd give you the low-down on Kitty and my grandad, Hatty,' he says. 'Mum and Dad think it's just so cool.'

'What's cool?'

'My grandad is going over to Kitty's for dinner. She must have worn him out. He told my parents he's only going because she's a poor old soul who needs company, but he went out and had a hair cut and bought some after-shave. He smells like a pine forest.'

'Victor, this is great.'

'There's one major problem, Hatty.'

'What?'

'It's my grandad's surname. Same as mine. It won't matter if they don't get serious. But if they did, you know, go crazy and get married, well . . . got to go now. You'll work it out.'

'Huh?' After I put the phone down I try to remember Arthur's surname. The cat next door lets out a throaty miaow while my brain is ticking. That's when I remember. Poor old Kitty could end up as Kitty Katt.

Saturday morning. Kitty comes bursting through our front door, running as though she's being chased by a hungry lion.

'Joe, Margaret, Hatty, Ron, Georgia, Harriet, Thomas, I'm in love.'

I rub my eyes and grab my dressing gown.

Kitty kisses Joe, then says very loudly, 'Love, I said love. Did anyone hear me?'

'I heard you, Kitty.' Mum comes wandering out of her bedroom. 'You said something about tea and toast. I'll just put the kettle on.'

Mum pads her way to the kitchen. I stretch myself into a semi-awake state and follow Kitty, who is skipping down the hall. 'How can you be in love? It's too soon, Kitty. And he's got a skinny windpipe. How can you love a man with a skinny windpipe?'

'I love him even with his skinny windpipe. That's what love is all about,' says Kitty.

Joe shakes his head. 'Mum, you romantic

old thing. But don't you fight all the time?'

'He's full of fire. We argue constantly. Just like your father, Joe. Arthur told me my food gave him indigestion. Silly man. Everyone knows that if you have a skinny windpipe you have to chew your food properly. That's his problem.'

Over tea and toast, I say to Kitty, 'Can you fit a cookery column into your hectic life?'

Kitty goes crackers when I tell her about having her very own cookery column.

'Kitty's Korner lives again,' she screams. 'What a hoot! I'm having such a time.'

'Are you sure about Arthur?' Mum asks her. 'I mean, you hardly know him. He could be a retired murderer for all we know. Aren't you jumping the gun?'

Kitty weeps with laughter at that. 'A retired murderer and I'm jumping the gun. Ha, ha.'

'Remember that awful man Hatty wrote to, pretending to be me?' says Mum. 'He sounded very refined, and he turned out to be serving time on a prison farm.'

'It's no good warning me. I'm high on love and I don't intend to hit Earth for some time. Still, I really appreciate your concern very much, Margaret.'

Mum smiles. She looks studiously into her tea, then carefully wipes crumbs away from her lips. 'I think I went overboard with you,

112

Kitty. I actually miss having you around. Not that I'm suggesting you spend your life here but, well, I do miss you.'

I look closely at Mum's nostrils. Not an inflatable dinghy in sight. Mum is telling the absolute truth.

Kitty's small yellow teeth gleam at us. 'I haven't been this happy since I had that huge fight with Joe's dad, when we didn't talk for a week and then made up.'

Chapter Eleven

On Sunday the sky is clear blue, with frothy white clouds. It looks like a vast ocean, with white yachts sailing on it.

Suzy comes over after breakfast. She's seen Mr Bates, and says he's very impressed with her advice on how to stop his five-year-old from painting the house purple. (Build him a cubby house and let him go mad. If that fails, Superglue his fingers together).

I happily hand over half the letters from my mail bag. She's going to take it all very seriously, she tells me. All those kids out there need her help. I nod. She also suggests we make up a cute card for fan letters instead of writing individually.

'Okay, it's not very personal, Hatty, but we can sign the cards. And it means *we* get to have a personal life. I know our fans will understand.'

After she goes, I punch the air happily. She's taking half the load. I can keep the Hotline going and have a life again. There's no doubt about it. I've given myself some top advice.

Kitty has already compiled a list of recipes for her column and Mum is talking about taking up a pottery course. She stared at Ron and Georgia yesterday and said, 'There could be a future in this. We might set up a stall at the markets, Joe, and sell garden gnomes. It would help pay for an overseas trip to see my relatives in England.'

Overseas trip. I think about that. I wonder if Raymond and I will ever travel overseas together? Maybe I should spend my savings on a trip to India instead, so I can speak to yogis about the meaning of life. Apart from being able to twist their bodies into impossible positions, they're supposed to be full of wisdom. On the other hand, I may drive them nuts. How much can a Yogi bear? Ha, ha.

'Gnomes,' says Mum, again. 'There's something rather quaint about them.'

'I thought you hated gernomees, Mum.'

'When did I say that?' says Mum, looking confused. 'I guess they've grown on me. Look at them, Hatty. They're rather sweet. At times, I could swear Ron and Georgia are actually smiling at each other.'

Joe's changing too. He gives Mum and I a choice. He needs at least one nervous habit, to survive. He can study his tooth pickings or go back to cracking his knuckles. We think hard and choose the latter. So, though he still diligently uses a toothpick, he cups one hand politely over his mouth. And he doesn't stare hypnotically at the mound of picked food particles on his plate any more.

He is now going through 'pick' withdrawal and drinks a lot of black coffee. 'It's very hard to break a habit, Hatty,' he tells me, pouring coffee down his throat. Then he glances at Aunt Harriet and Thomas.

'I don't talk to them when you're around,' I say defensively. 'But I can't give them up.'

'I understand Hatty,' says Joe. 'Everyone's entitled to at least one nervous habit.' He gives his knuckles a crack for good measure. 'Have you noticed how your mother's nostrils widen when she's telling fibs.'

'No,' I say, innocently. 'Imagine that.'

Right now, Mum's at the local pottery shop. She's talking to them about making garden gnomes.

I go to my bedroom, put on my new, strategically faded jeans and a t-shirt, then change the t-shirt for another one that is loose-fitting. I briefly stare at myself in the mirror. Hair shiny. Good. Skin clear. Good. Eyes – steady but a bit miserable-looking.

'Going out,' I call to Joe. 'Tell Mum I'll be back later.'

I hop off the bus at Watsons Bay. The street leading to the hotel is crowded. The adjoining park is filled with kids chasing each other, couples walking under trees and families sitting on large blankets, pigging out. The bay itself is beautiful. Lots of boats bob around the navy-blue water and people stroll along the pier leading out to where the ferry docks.

I turn in at the hotel. People sit eating fish and chips. Small kids slurp on lemonade.

He's there with his dad's group. Raymond. His dad is belting out 'Satin Doll' on the clarinet. The guitarist nods in time to the music and plucks strings. The drummer taps on the drums. There, sitting at the piano, his head bent low over the notes, is Raymond. I find myself a table and order a Coke.

Somewhere in amongst the crowd, Suzy is probably curled up with Giles. But I don't want to be with them today. I'll just sit here quietly and listen. Let the music seep through my pores.

I drink slowly. Raymond occasionally looks up from the piano and stares at the crowd. I want to tell everyone there to shut up. Stop guzzling your fish and chips. You there with the mouth like a tunnel, stop talking. You there with the zinc cream on your nose, stop wriggling and sit still. You kids, stop squealing at each other and listen. You won't hear music like this anywhere else.

I am halfway through my drink when the familiar, haunting strains of 'Sweet Georgia Brown' start. I put my drink down, and sit there, tapping time to the music. Is it still my song, our song, Raymond?

There's a mass of tangled rope knotting my stomach. If this continues I may end up strangling myself.

Sadly, the music has lost something. The zippy beat isn't there. 'Sweet Georgia Brown' sounds more like 'Melancholy Georgia Brown'. The rest of the band try to liven it up, but Raymond is playing slowly and each note is strained.

His face is serious, his eyes dark and moody. He scans the crowd as his hands move lightly and mechanically over the piano keys. I watch him. Hey, it's me. Hatty. This way. Look this way.

Raymond lowers his head and plays a wrong note. I wince. I see him squint slightly as he looks up, then peers this way and that, past the barbeque area, sifting methodically through family groups and couples.

Suddenly, he scores a bullseye!

As our eyes meet, I see him mouth the word. 'Hatty?'

I raise my glass in a salute to him, and smile.

Suddenly, 'Sweet Georgia Brown' takes off. And now, it isn't 'Sweet Georgia Brown'. It's 'Hip Georgia Brown'. It's ... it's ...

The music is magic. Even Raymond's dad swivels his clarinet around and stares at Raymond. Raymond's hands are running over the piano at top speed, even though he's not looking at the keys. His eyes are on me and his smile broadens.

Raymond says something to his dad. He jumps off the stage and runs to me, pulling me to my feet, and suddenly we're dancing. Between tables. Right past a startled Suzy and Giles. I'm swirling and twirling. He's holding me and touching my hair and saying, 'I've missed you Hatty, and I've been an idiot.'

He kisses me passionately on the lips. I kiss him back. My Raymond. The blurred crowd cheers and suddenly I'm thinking of Great Aunt Harriet and Thomas. If they'd have just made up. If only ...

Later, we walk along the small pier facing the bay. The afternoon sun is sinking beneath the horizon, and the sky looks like frothy pink meringue.

At the end of the pier I see a couple. The woman is wearing a long silky dress, and her hair is parted in the centre. The guy is dressed in one of those old-fashioned suits. The man has his arms around her. Even from here you can see that they're in love.

It can't be . . . I shake my head in disbelief, blink and suddenly . . . they've gone. Clean disappeared.

It's that crazy imagination of mine and those last blurred rays of sunlight fogging my vision.

Raymond puts his arm around me. 'I hear they've planted new trees at Watsons Bay Park, Hatty, lots and lots of them.'

He winks at me and takes my hand.

About the Author

Moya Simons lives in Sydney and has two grown-up daughters, Suzy and Tamie. Moya spends a lot of time writing and says that marshmallows and chocolate help to inspire her.

While she doesn't have a picture of Great Aunt Harriet to talk to (like Hatty), she does admit to singing to her pot plants. And do they sing back and offer advice when needed? Well, of course. Don't all pot plants do that?

Moya's other books are *Iggy from Outer Space*, *Sit Down, Mum, There's Something I've Got to Tell You*, *Dead Meat!*, *Dead Average!*, *Dead Worried!*, *Fourteen Something* and *Spacenapped!*

**IF YOU ENJOYED *HATTY'S HOTLINE*,
WHY NOT READ ANOTHER WICKEDLY
FUNNY STORY ABOUT HATTY?**

> *Sit down, Mum, there's
> something I've got to tell you*
> MOYA SIMONS

In this madcap, fast-moving story, Hatty
decides that her divorced mum needs a
love-life. She sees an ad in the paper and
reckons that Morris would be just right
for her mum. So what if her mother
isn't interested right now? She will
be sooner or later . . .

Hatty writes to Morris, pretending to be
her mum. The results are hilarious!

MORE GREAT READING FROM PUFFIN

☆☆☆☆☆☆☆☆☆☆☆☆☆☆☆☆☆☆☆☆☆☆☆☆

Hating Alison Ashley   Robin Klein

'There was one kid, Alison Ashley, and because no one was sitting next to me, Miss Belmont put Alison Ashley there. And from the first day I hated her.'

So says Erica Yurken when the oh-so-perfect Alison Ashley turns up at Barringa East Primary . . . A bestselling, very funny story from this popular author.

Shortlisted for the 1985 CBC Book of the Year Award. Winner of the Young Australians' Best Book Award (YABBA) 1987. Winner of the Kids' Own Australian Literature Awards (KOALA) 1987.

Halfway Across the Galaxy and Turn Left   Robin Klein

The hilarious account of what happens to a family banished from their planet, Zyrgon, when they have to spend a period of exile on Earth.

Shortlisted for the 1986 CBC Book of the Year Award, and now an exciting television series.

Turn Right For Zyrgon   Robin Klein

The funny and totally unexpected antics of that weird family from Zyrgon continue. This time, they return to their home planet and find that things aren't quite the same any more.

MORE GREAT READING FROM PUFFIN

☆☆☆☆☆☆☆☆☆☆☆☆☆☆☆☆☆☆☆☆☆☆☆☆☆☆☆☆

The White Guinea-Pig   Ursula Dubosarsky

When Geraldine is entrusted with the care of her friend's white guinea-pig, Alberta, and when that guinea-pig mysteriously disappears, it is the beginning of Geraldine's growing up, and everything in her life changes.

Winner of the 1994 New South Wales State Literary Children's Book Award and the 1994 Victorian Premier's Literary Award, and shortlisted for the 1994 CBC Children's Book of the Year Award – Older Readers.

The First Book of Samuel   Ursula Dubosarsky

On his twelfth birthday, Samuel Cass disappeared . . . A subtle and resonant story of identity and growth, by a truly original author.

Bruno and the Crumhorn   Ursula Dubosarsky

When Bruno is forced to learn a cumbersome, medieval musical instrument, little does he know the unlikely chain of events that will follow! Another highly original story from this talented author.

MORE GREAT READING FROM PUFFIN

☆☆☆☆☆☆☆☆☆☆☆☆☆☆☆☆☆☆☆☆☆☆☆☆☆☆☆☆

The Lake at the End of the World   Caroline Macdonald

It is 2025 and the world has been cleared of all life by a chemical disaster. But then Diana meets Hector . . .

Winner of the 1989 Alan Marshall Award, named an Honour Book in the 1989 CBC Book of the Year Awards and shortlisted for the NSW Premier's Award. Runner-up for the 1990 Guardian Children's Fiction Award.

Speaking to Miranda   Caroline Macdonald

On her quest to discover the truth about her mother's death seventeen years ago, Ruby gradually uncovers the answers to her questions – and much more besides.

Shortlisted for the 1991 CBC Book of the Year Award for Older Readers and the 1991 New Zealand AIM Children's Book Award.